Titles by Paula V. Ha

Forever Lost
The Unforeseen Rescue

A Daughter's Justice
Paula V. Hardin

Cover design by: Michael Hardin Sr.

First Edition.

www.paulavhardin.com

Acknowledgments
First I want to always thank my husband for
all his support and love. Thank you so much to
my editor Becky Highnote who keeps me going,
and pushes me for more pages. She's amazing

and I'm forever grateful. If you're in need of
a great editor who also loves to read here is
her email: bextruk@gmail.com

A special thank you goes out to Kimberly Fry
for helping me come up with my title. She's
also my beta reader and I love her endlessly.

Chapter 1

"All charges have been dropped due to lack of evidence from the District Attorney's office. Mr. Joseph Gambino is remanded back to the custody of the Orleans Parish Criminal Sheriff's Department to be released." The judge pounded his gavel against the sounding block to quiet the spectators' angry reaction to the verdict.

New Orleans defense attorney Merrick Hardin gladly gathered her papers and shoved them into her briefcase. Goosebumps rose at the back of her neck making her shiver when she felt someone staring. Deep down she knew who it was, and it made her knees go weak. Merrick forced herself not to turn toward sexy Command Sergeant Major Stone, knowing she would see disappointment in his eyes. He made her feel things she wasn't prepared to examine too closely. Why did it matter so much what he thought of her? It was really too late anyway because after this he probably thought like the others which made her feel exceptionally alone.

She felt numb. She had won, but there was no honor in the victory. It left a bitter taste in her mouth. In her mind she knew it wasn't over, not for Gambino. All that mattered now was making sure that the witness, Major Stone, was protected at all cost.

"You killed my boy, Gambino. You shouldn't be allowed to go free." Merrick heard the anguish in the father's voice. It made her sick inside and her heart heavy. She fought against the anguish.

"You!" she heard the father say. Merrick knew it was directed at her. Her stomach knotted up because she knew she wasn't going to like what was coming.

"You're Satan's spawn. You're here doing his dirty work. Killing off the innocents and helping the guilty."

His angered voice made her physically sick inside. Merrick felt her stomach roll.

She couldn't turn and look at the family or she'd lose it.

The briefcase of cash sitting in her safe didn't seem worth it. If the people understood her method of justice, it would be perfect. They couldn't understand because they had no clue. She pushed her fingers through her hair, feeling a migraine coming on.

The case against Gambino had been stressful. She had worked long hours to ensure his release. She wondered why the mayor himself hounded her every move. His motives were skeptical to say the least. Rumor had it the mayor was dirty, that he put his hands in many dealings going down in the metropolitan area. The trial was finally over, and relief flooded every cell of her body. She was exhausted, but sleep had to wait. She needed to make sure the eyewitness was safe. He was military, but Gambino was dirty, a leader of the New Orleans mafia.

Merrick pushed her way through the crowd of angry people who stood outside the courthouse. News reporters crowded her, shoving microphones in her face. Different voices threw questions at her, waiting for answers. They hated her with a vengeance, and none of them understood why she defended these criminals.`

Being the center of attention was not something she looked forward to, but she tried to satisfy the reporters with an evasive yes or no. Merrick walked faster, keeping her back straight. The faces were angry, yelling, and someone from behind felt brave enough to shove her. She paid them no attention because any reaction could start a scene with her being the main attraction.

When someone behind her pulled her hair, she secretly thanked her lucky stars it was only a wig. She grinned, thinking what a surprise they would get if they saw the real her.

From a distance, she spotted her 2014 red Aston Martin roadster. As she reached the curb and the safety of her car with her keys in her hand, prepared to unlock the door, she froze in horror.

She gasped and took a step back, appalled that someone had spray-painted the word "BITCH" on the side of her baby. Merrick looked around, wondering if whoever had done this was still watching. A crowd surrounded her and her car, preventing her from leaving. A huge man beat his fist against the hood of her car. Merrick was livid. She wanted to scream, "*Fuck you*," but she didn't because she realized it would only give them satisfaction in knowing they got to her, not to mention the media was out in full force.

She yanked the door open and thought, *How dare someone try to intimidate me!* As she slammed the door closed, Merrick held back the angry tears and threw her purse across to the passenger seat.

The car roared to life with its V-12 engine, giving the crowd their only warning to move. The car jumped into traffic, causing nearby cars to get out the way. *How could someone spray paint an Aston Martin?* she wondered in disgust. Why did she put herself though all the headaches? Deep down she knew why. Merrick had lost her father when she was young. Her mother had struggled to provide and protect their small family. Merrick did this to protect her family and to give the people of the city a fighting chance at a normal life.

With the economy deteriorating daily, more people found themselves without jobs and homeless. Lost in the loopholes for aid or without enough to survive, families were now living under bridges and alleyways, fighting to survive.

Merrick was determined that no child living on the streets, homeless, or orphaned was forgotten. Behind the scenes, she bought

8

old warehouses and turned then into safe
havens and new beginnings.

When she found a quiet place to park,
she pulled over and killed the engine. Her
fingers flicked a lever on the console. When
it opened, she pulled out her goggles. She had
designed these bad boys and made them herself.
No one knew who she really was, not the people
of New Orleans, not the judges, and least of
all, not the bad guys. Feeling rebellious, she
realized she was glad at the moment they
didn't.

Merrick positioned the goggles against
her face without slipping the leather strap
over her head. She adjusted the aperture
displaying the past hour through the lenses.

While constructing the goggles into her
steam punk fashion a few years ago, she had
added a piece of rare mineral she had found
while metal detecting. She personally believed
it was a chunk from a meteor. When she tried
them for the first time, she was stunned to
find she could see into the future and into
the past. It only allowed a timeframe of
around eight hours on a good day, depending on
the weather.

The vertigo-like dizziness made her
upset stomach curl a little more. She held
fast to the goggles, knowing this feeling
would pass. Much like someone walking from out
of a fog, she watched the scene unfold.

An unmarked black van pulled up, and the
side door slid open. Two masked assailants
jumped out and painted her door within
seconds, jumped back in the waiting vehicle,
and drove off. Merrick turned her head trying
to see behind the van, but of course, it had
no license plate.

She set the goggles back into their
hiding place and drove to her home near City
Park. It had been a long day, and she was
tired as she pulled into the driveway on the
side of her house and turned the car off. It
was already dark due to daylight savings time.
Her motion sensor was on before its time,

sending goosebumps down her spine. It spooked her a little after today's events.

She opened her car door and stepped out. A huge possum jumped from the garbage can, knocking the lid to the ground with a loud explosion. Merrick pulled her gun from under her long skirt. Her heart was beating loudly in her ears. She aimed the gun, following the sudden movement to see a mother possum scurry behind the bushes, carrying a load of babies on its back. Merrick holstered her gun, more than a little relieved. She leaned inside and quickly grabbed her purse and briefcase, slinging them out of the way as she shut the car door.

With the sound of the door shutting behind her, Merrick started walking toward the house. Before she could call it a night, she had to do one thing. Deep inside she felt an urgent need to hurry, even though her body screamed for a hot shower and bed.

Something drew her attention toward the entrance of the house. Merrick stared straight into the eyes of Joseph Gambino. He was lurking in the shadows where she almost didn't see him, and he was holding flowers as if he was about to take her out on a date. The nerve of the man made her grit her teeth. She stopped; her heart jumped to her throat. Prickles of uneasiness ran down her spine, accompanied by now sweaty palms. The gun against her leg suddenly felt heavy. She wished it were in her hand.

Merrick fumbled with her purse, bending her head slightly away to take a quick breath and put her game face on. At the same time she tried to get a quick look around to see who else might be lurking in the shadows. Gambino was never without his henchmen, and she didn't want someone sneaking up behind her. She needed to be smart about how to handle the situation.

Before she could utter a word, she watched him approach. The way he looked at her gave Merrick the creeps. If he thought he could come here and push roses under her nose and think he was going to make her one of his dumb bimbos, then he was on crack. His confidence was about to get a dose of reality. She could almost see the wheels turning in his head. His game might work on some airhead looking for a good time, but not this time, not from this girl, that's for damn sure. She cringed in disgust and fear. Her body trembled slightly from being caught off-guard, but what she really wanted to do was shove the roses down his throat. The audacity of the man was absolutely horrifying. Instead she forced herself to accept the flowers when he pushed them at her.

"I wanted to come thank you in person for today," Gambino offered.

"You came to me because I'm the best, and you paid me to do a job. There is no need for thanks, Mr. Gambino." She made sure she addressed him properly, professionally. "But I thank you for the roses." Merrick moved slightly, making herself stand tall, confident, and determined.

"I'm afraid you caught me at a bad time. I'm actually only here for a quick moment. If you need to confer with me, call my secretary in the morning and make the necessary arrangements. Good evening, Mr. Gambino." Merrick gave him that look, the attorney glare indicating she meant business.

At that precise moment, two police units pulled into her driveway, blocking her in, and four officers exited the vehicles. "Oh, great. Now what?" Merrick grumbled aloud, but thought silently, *Thank you, Newton and Fusion.*

"We received a call of a break in. I need to see some identification," one of the officers stated.

"My name is Merrick Hardin, and this is my house," she offered while digging in her purse for her license.

"I know you." One of the officers pointed. "You're Gambino, Joseph Gambino. Your face is all over the news. The people in this city are up in arms over your release." The officer shook his head.

Once the officer gave her license back, she wanted to escape inside, make her getaway so to speak. Merrick whispered to the officer to walk Gambino to his car nice and easy, friendly like as if he didn't realize what was happening.

The officer nodded his head, and Merrick slipped inside quietly, locking the door behind her. She leaned against the door, her legs a little shaky. Her lifestyle was going to be the death of her yet.

Merrick automatically disabled the alarm. Still, she listened intently for any sound or movement. Once the verdict made the news, Merrick mentally prepared herself for the backlash effect from the media. Her face would be plastered on the front page of the local newspaper. The ripple effect would generate gossip on all levels of hatred, mistrust, and rebellion. With her line of work and being a woman, she always put a lot of effort into her safety so after such cases she took time off to regroup and allow the media to lose interest.

Her purse and briefcase dropped to the floor as she kicked off her designer pumps with a heavy sigh of relief. She pulled off the wig and the cap that kept her hair from escaping and leaned over at the waist, shaking out her black dreads.

The closest entrance to the house was by the portable aluminum car shelter stationed in the alley between neighbors. Immediately inside was the kitchen. The laundry room was through the door on the far wall.

She walked into the laundry room, feeling the weight of the day pull her down. Her muscles screamed with tension. She pulled off the expensive Chanel blazer and let it fall to the floor. Next, she peeled off her matching long skirt, revealing colorful tattoos down her legs. Her blouse followed, showing more tattoos up her back. The professional attire expected from a highly paid defense attorney was not really her style.

Against the far wall hidden within the shelves, she punched in the code for the separate security system. Merrick entered the basement, wearing nothing but her underwear. She was confident she was safe inside with special security setup to alert her if anyone trespassed.

The flanking wall to the basement held a closet full of clothes embellished with pieces of leather, metal with nuts and bolts, or some other kind of hardware. This was her lifestyle, not the straight-laced well-dressed attorney she portrayed to the public. Merrick joined a group of wonderful, talented people who loved and supported the art of steam punk with gatherings and events. This was where she could be herself. It was where she was the happiest. The largest of them all, which she waited for all year long, was the Steam punk World Fair.

The clank of metal made her turn towards Fusion, her artificial intelligence jaguar. She had built it by hand with polished black metal and copper fittings. Merrick was mystified, as the big cat appeared very real, almost life-like. From time to time, she only needed a little oil. "Hey girl, it's good to be home," she rubbed the top of Fusion's head as she brushed up against Merrick's leg like a regular house cat.

She dressed quickly in a black form-fitting woman's shirt with elastic in the neck, sleeveless, with a steam punk dragon across the front. Over the shirt, she added a skinny camel-colored shrug with hand-painted brass buttons. Handmade, stretchy, super comfortable, black skinny-fit pants with five belt loops and a fat belt came next.

She handpicked all the items with care because when she put herself in danger, she needed items to move with her, not against her. Her knee-high, black leather lace-up-the-front, pointed toe, ass-kicking boots finished off her outfit, and she added large brass globe earrings and matching goggles.

Merrick went to the floor-to-ceiling mirror to check out her outfit and shook out her dreads. With great care she pulled out her brown contacts. It was a constant reminder of something foreign being in her eyes. Merrick blinked a few times feeling a sense of peace as she glanced at her reflection, revealing ocean green eyes. She stood there for a moment to remind herself of who she was and what she really stood for no matter what others whispered.

No one knew who Merrick Hardin really was except for her mother. Her hidden identity kept her family safe. Anyone looking into her background would pull up nothing. Except for Gambino, who now knew where she lived. Cursing under her breath, she knew she couldn't dwell on that at the moment. When it was time to leave, she needed to make sure the coast was clear and no one was lingering close by.

She turned away from her reflection and walked over to another section of the basement where her cycle sat next to her workbench. "Thank you, Newton and Fusion, for sending the cavalry to my rescue."

Her cycle wasn't a normal everyday bike but built in steam punk style full of extras. Merrick was proud of herself, having done all the modifications herself. She actually named her cycle Newton. Pushed and bullied to race against some of the top cyclists in the underworld of steampunkers, she won. Now she was looking forward to this year because Merrick (or Jynx as she was known on the steam punk circuit) wanted to prove skill wasn't a fluke, but she earned her win. *He's my mystery as well. I don't question it. I just enjoy the benefits of having my two sidekicks*, she thought.

"Good evening, Mistress, I'm glad to see you're safe and sound. I called in an intruder distress call to the police department, trying give you some interference," the voice came from the cycle. Its deep male voice sounded almost human, not like what was heard on the computer speak-to-text thing. "We're all set to go."

"Could you scan the area farther out to make sure we don't have any unwanted spies hiding out? I don't want to be caught again unprepared."

"All is clear, Mistress. Gambino and his men and the police are no longer in the vicinity," Newton replied.

Fusion, the jag, purred in readiness.

The engine started with a muted roar of power as Merrick straddled the seat, patting the tank lovingly as she adjusted her body. The bike glowed and pulsed like a heartbeat between her legs. She never installed any equipment for him to glow, but it only did it when she touched the bike out of love. "Twelve thirty-eight First Street," she instructed. "We need to go check on the eyewitness to make sure he's safe. Fusion, are you ready for some exercise, girl?"

The previous night, Merrick had sent the files to Newton. The bike functioned on its own. He could program himself and communicate with Fusion. Merrick had placed some of the rare minerals she had found from a meteor crater in Arizona she had visited. After sneaking into the crater, she used her metal detector deep down at the base, and a few times the metal detector signal alerted her to a finding. When she picked up certain pieces of the minerals at they glowed and made her hand tingle. Something made her add the mineral pieces when she created Fusion and Newton. She couldn't explain it, but it was the only explanation she could rationalize. None of it made any sense, which was why her private life remained private.

Merrick knew with a certainty she would be in the papers in the morning. She wouldn't put it past Gambino to quiet the eyewitness permanently, so Merrick needed to get to him

first and make sure Stone was safe. Nothing
could happen to him because the news people,
newspapers, and every tabloid would have a
field day at her expense. Not to mention she
didn't want his death on her conscience.

What the people didn't understand was
that she saved the taxpayers thousands of
dollars. Joseph Gambino was now on her list,
but first she had to get to the eyewitness
Stone's residence. Although Stone had military
training, Gambino was a force to be reckoned
with, and Stone probably thought he was
Superman or something.

The cycle hummed softly down the streets
until she turned down First Street. "Mistress,
there is gun fire at the address of the
eyewitness." The cycle pulled over at the
curb.

Chapter 2

"Fusion, go protect Stone," Merrick directed orders with a steady voice. "Newton, can you give me a survey of the area and show me the eyewitness?"

A holographic display came up from a small compartment, and within seconds, she watched the scene unfold.

"Damn! I need to get in there." The motorcycle raced down the street. Someone with a mask hiding his face and dressed in black ran to intercede her intervention. Her cycle Newton never slowed, but when he was close enough, he rose up on his front tire and swung his rear-end around, sending the man airborne until he slammed into a parked car.

Merrick jumped off and ran alongside Newton who erected a protective shield against the flying bullets while he guided himself next to Merrick for protection.

From the sides of her legs, Merrick pulled two modified collapsible police batons and slung them out, forcing the metal out from the handles. On each stick, she pushed a button driving out little sharp spikes to lock in place. The batons couldn't kill, but they could put a man down quickly.

Two men in black rushed her from opposite directions. Merrick swung the batons in perfect symphony, pivoting on the balls of her feet, beating the men unmercifully with quick blows to the body. She jumped up, and raising her feet, kicked one man square in the chest and sent him flying backwards.

Her dreads swung out around her head as she turned in a circle. She bashed the batons against the second intruder's body knocking him unconscious. A car exploded, sending debris from the vehicle and anything close by to litter the street. Flames roared from the remains of the automobile, sending out massive waves of heat. Merrick knew Gambino's thugs were responsible for the damage. She had arrived too late.

Merrick searched the yard, down the street, and the neighbors' driveways, looking for her eyewitness. "Fusion," she called over the roar of the fire. There was no answer.

"Fusion is fine and protecting Stone." The male voice from her cycle interrupted Merrick. "He's down, shot multiple times and in shock. Fusion is trying to stop the bleeding as much as she can until you arrive."

When Merrick reached Fusion, she could see blood pooling from Stone's wounds, but Fusion lay on top of him, using a force field around the two of them to keep them safe from attack and gunfire. Merrick's heart slammed against her chest when she saw that he was unconscious. All that blood was his, and it was her fault. He was not going to die on her watch.

Newton, the motorcycle, opened a compartment from the side of his cycle where a small cab unfolded and assembled.

Merrick had to drag Stone's heavy body into the cab, trying to hurry as the police sirens approached. The hospital wasn't a safe place for Stone. He would be an easy target for Gambino's men to come to finish what they had started. "I'll have to take him home," she told Newton and Fusion.

My basement will be the best place to keep him safe, she thought as Merrick straddled her bike. Newton ejected an invisibly screen as they sped by the patrol cars, leaving behind a great mess of debris and dead bodies. They rode out undetected.

With the protection barriers she had created against intruders at her home, God himself couldn't break into her basement. For the first time she glanced down at the eyewitness. He sure was easy on the eyes. Black-headed men had always been her weakness. The moment she had touched his lean body to drag him into the cab she had noticed his perfection. He was all muscle and damn beautiful. With her imagination running wild, she would bet her paycheck he was cut like a Greek god.

Merrick moved to the secret entrance of the basement. Before entering, Newton used his heat sensors to scan the property and surrounding areas. Once clear, Merrick entered the basement and ordered Newton to lock the place down.

The large basement was well equipped with a full kitchen and a bathroom with a shower. She kept it supplied with food and water. When she was home, Merrick spent most of her time in the basement with her wide-screen television, computer, and a daybed for the many nights she'd never made it upstairs. If need be, she could live here for a few months.

Being a woman, one wouldn't expect her basement to be equipped with blowtorches, welding machines, and all the other necessary tools for Merrick's Victorian, sci-fi creations. Merrick collected all kinds of metals and other odds and ends people usually cast out. One never knew the value of an object.

She had installed a vault in the wall to keep the cash she extorted from the criminals until she could find a place to donate the money. She discreetly donated money to different organizations and helped the homeless, especially the battered women's shelter. Every area needed money, but she couldn't give to them all or the public would wonder where the cash was coming from. They might discover her secret.

She made sure she had plenty of weapons and obviously was fully supplied with ammunition. Merrick needed it for her nightlife of fighting crime, taking down the very criminals the government let slip through the system. Although it was more than she could personally handle, Merrick was determined to give it her best shot. Her two companions helped immensely, and she knew without them she could not accomplish as much as she did.

Merrick didn't have many friends, especially co-workers. She lived a life of ridicule from other lawyers and the people of New Orleans. Many were just plain jealous of her expertise as a lawyer, and some thought she was on the take from the criminals she got exonerated. Her friends were those who knew her as herself, mostly the steam punk community.

She smiled down at the unconscious eyewitness. She already regretted bringing him here, but her hand had been forced. She blamed herself for getting him shot. This was a first of firsts.

Her attention jerked back to Stone's face as he started to stir and moan in pain. Merrick's heart twisted in guilt as she slid off her cycle and moved to his side.

"You're safe," she tried to assure him, as she slid her arm under his armpits and tried to haul him out of the cab of the bike. "Come on, big guy, I need a little help here." The muscles in her legs strained to support his weight. Damn, she could smell his cologne. Merrick gritted her teeth. Even with his help, it was difficult to maneuver him towards the daybed.

The air rushed out of her lungs in a frustrated gasp as they twisted and fell. He landed on top of her, pinning her to the bed. Merrick took a gulp of air and tried to roll him over. Nothing happened. "Try to help me, big guy," she grunted. The weight of his body left her gasping for air.

Merrick detected movement, a loud grunt of pain, and then she was free. Air rushed in her lungs as she turned towards him. Somehow, he must have found the strength to roll onto his back. Blood gushed from under his shirt.

Merrick didn't waste any time; she wasn't sure how much blood Stone had lost. "I'm only trying to help you. I'll need to take the bullets out. Do you understand?"

"Yes." There was a pause, a loud breath. "Do what you have to." The words came out in a hiss of agony. His hand snaked out and grabbed her arm. "My briefcase. Did you get my briefcase? And no hospitals, I'll be dead by morning."

Before she could reply, he collapsed. She knew she hadn't grabbed any briefcase, but Fusion strolled over with a stainless steel case in her mouth. "Good girl." Merrick immediately began to cut his shirt and jeans away with a pair of scissors, careful not to touch his skin. She'd worry about the briefcase later.

It took over an hour to extract all the bullets from his body. One was lodged in his shoulder, another one had grazed his side, and the last one went straight through his inner thigh, barely missing a main artery. Recently he'd been shot close to his heart, leaving behind a fresh pink scar. Absently Merrick traced the edge thinking this was probably from the assassin at the cafe. The large gash on his rib cage showed he'd been in a knife fight. At least that wound was old and faded.

The tattoo on his shoulder matched the Special Forces decal, but she'd already known this from the information provided during the trial.

By the time she finished cleaning and stitching his wounds, it was almost morning. Her clothes were full of blood, and she was exhausted. Not to mention the last time she had eaten anything was yesterday morning, and that had just been a bowl of cereal. Luckily, she'd already scheduled the day off, expecting all kinds of backlash over the verdict.

She quickly jumped in the shower and put a pair of men's baggy pajama bottoms with the top of them curled over. She grabbed her favorite old tank shirt she always slept in and left the bathroom. The overstuffed leather recliner would have to do. Fusion, who usually slept in the daybed with her, climbed on top of her legs, curled up, and shut her eyes.

Merrick didn't even flinch. The cat's weight felt more like a security blanket. She was asleep in seconds.

Merrick opened her eyes wearily, struggling against the deep sleep trying to drag her back down. After the night of getting up and down to check on her patient, another hour sounded heavenly. As soon as her brain caught up, she burst from the chair and turned towards her patient but stopped dead.

He was awake and watching her. Fusion was cuddled up next to him. How long the jaguar been there Merrick had no clue. "Good morning. How do you feel?" she forced the words from her morning-breath mouth, trying to hide the sudden jealousy.

"Sore as hell. I don't remember much of what happened. When I'm not thinking about it, I catch a glimpse of you on the edge of my consciousness, but I can't hold on to the image."

"Give it some time. It'll come back to you soon enough. I wouldn't try force it, but someone tried to kill you last night. You told me not to take you to the hospital because if I did you'd be dead by morning." There was no reason to tell him who she really was or why she had been there to begin with.

Merrick had never run into this kind of situation. No one had ever needed her protection in the past. She'd have to be careful to keep her real identity separate. When she looked into his eyes, she knew he was dangerous to her on a completely different level.

People didn't like her, at least not the lawyer part of her. Everyone thought she was on the take. She did take the criminals' money, but she used that money to help the city. The criminals she dealt with were rich and demented, and she used their own cash flow to destroy them.

Merrick had always considered herself a geeky girl, a loner. Now she was babysitting this hunk, and parts of her wanted more. To know this about herself scared the daylights out of her.

"Where am I?" His deep voice broke into her thoughts.

"How long have I been here?" Stone tried to rise up on his elbow, but he fell backwards, grunting in pain.

"You're safe," Merrick replied, "as long as you don't try to leave." Merrick rushed to the bed and checked his bandages. "You need to be still, or your wounds will start to bleed again." Her fingers ran over this shoulder and against the side of his ribs. Her gaze went to the inside of his thigh.

"I'm not a doctor, but I did manage to get the bullet out. The other wounds were clean." She removed her hand, fighting the urge to keep touching him. Instead, she smiled self-consciously, shoving her hands behind her back.

"You just rest, and anything you need is right here. There is a full kitchen and bathroom, cable television and internet. I'd caution you not to call anyone to tell them you're safe, like your wife or girlfriend or even your parents. You can endanger all of them if the people after you have their phones tapped.

"Do you have any questions?" Merrick watched Fusion creep up and put her nose under his hand for attention. She could kick herself for the jealousy and all the questions this was going to bring about.

"Yes, I do actually. For starters how did I get here? Who are you? Then I might add a few more. It all depends on your answers." Stone watched her blush.

"You don't remember anything at all?" Merrick watched Stone's face. "Seriously?" Skepticism filled her words before she could prevent it. "I apologize if I sound rude, but I'm having a hard time believing that." When he didn't say anything. Anyway, with a little help from my friends, I brought you here." She smiled and nodded her head towards Fusion.

"Meet Fusion, my mechanical jaguar. She thinks she's real."

"I thought I was hallucinating when she jumped up next to me when I woke up. What makes her work? Batteries?" Stone absentmindedly stroked the cat's head.

"You can call me Jynx." Merrick wasn't about to give him her real name. No way was she putting herself out there like that. She caught his smile, how his cheeks dimpled. She felt her knees go weak.

Her stomach growled. Maybe she should make them breakfast. She turned to ask. "No!" Merrick's panicked shout came across full of authority when he attempted to stand. "You're going to rip out your stitches." She caught the way her voice came across. She put her hands against his chest trying to catch him as his body pitched forward awkwardly. "You're in no shape to go anywhere." His skin was warm, his muscular hard body sent sparks of desire through her body.

"Please lie back down," the catch in her voice sounded full of concern. He pulled off something no one had ever accomplished. She never let anyone get close to her. Her reaction to him was something new, and she wasn't sure how to handle it. "Trust me, you're safe here." She jerked her fingers away feeling a sizzle of electricity spark her fingertips. She quickly glanced down at her nails, expecting to see them singed. "As long as you follow the rules and don't go upstairs."

"It's not me I'm worried about," Stone rebutted her concern with some of his own.

Distracted by the zing in her fingertips, she didn't hear what he said. "What did you say?"

"Nothing."

"Are you hungry? I can fix us some breakfast, or lunch," she said looking at her watch and noticing the time. Merrick changed the path of their conversation, turning towards the kitchen. She grabbed the remote

for the TV and tossed it to him. "Find
something good to watch. It's my day off."

"Thank you, breakfast sounds great.
Jynx?" He waited for her to turn. "I really
appreciate everything you have done for me."

In the kitchen with her back to him,
Merrick could hear the different sounds from
him flicking through the channels.

"Hey Jynx, tell your husband I love the
setup of this place. It's well thought out.
Did he have the cycle and the cat custom
made?"

"I do not have a husband or a
boyfriend." Her sarcastic reply shot out of
her mouth. "Everything you see," she pointed
around the basement, "I did myself. I custom
built Newton and Fusion, and I've made a lot
of other stuff." Merrick had to bite her
tongue from telling him off. It was there on
the tip of her tongue, but she fought against
allowing her attitude to erupt. "I'm sorry for
mouthing off, but damn, why does a woman have
to have a man around to have certain things?"

The disappointment hit a nerve because
he had automatically assumed a man put her
garage together. Somehow the comment coming
from him really made her sensitive. She heard
the sharp edge of her tone at her smart-ass
remarks to his off-handed compliment. It was
rude of her, but damn, she couldn't stop
herself if she tried.

Merrick moved around in the kitchen,
mentally kicking her own ass for reacting the
way she did. She forced herself to pull
herself together. She could hear one of the
broadcasters for ABC news announcing the
weather and another voice gave the rundown
over sports. Before she could utter a word,
she heard a broadcaster say, "Breaking news.
Last night's tragic event left one
neighborhood in chaos." The station proceeded
to show footage of the burning cars and a tree
from where Stone had been attacked.

It appeared to Merrick as if the
newsman's words seemed to point an invisible

finger at her. Merrick's legs wanted to give out on her as she stood in her kitchen, horrified at the details streaming across the screen of her television.

The nightmare continued playing across the screen, "The District Attorney's office has lost their eyewitness from protective custody. The authorities are following leads. There is speculation of foul play. If anyone has any information, please call, one eight hundred..."

"They're talking about you," Stone burst out.

Guiltily, she quickly turned away and almost dropped the two plates in her hands. Determined, Merrick straightened her spine until she reached him.

Because she was not prepared for his statement and didn't know how to explain it, Merrick ignored his outburst and redirected the conversation. "After you eat, I'll help you to the bathroom so you can take a shower. I have some men's pajama bottoms you can wear for now. Later I'll go out and pick up some jeans and a couple of shirts and some shoes. I'll need to get your sizes, and while you're in the shower, I'll change the sheets on the bed and remove the bloody ones."

Standing there with the plate in her hand, she silently wished he'd take the hint and not push for answers she couldn't give him. Merrick smiled tentatively, holding her breath and waiting. When the corner of his mouth smirked into a grin, Merrick relaxed.

"Tell me about Fusion," Stone implored.

"I can't. There is nothing really to tell." She shrugged self-consciously. Merrick didn't want to discuss the mechanics of her pieces. The fact that the jaguar had gone sweet on him really didn't sit well with her either, and she felt another twinge of jealousy. Merrick couldn't really be angry when she herself was crushing on Stone. He made her feel all womanly and awkward.

"I'm a geeky girl at heart. I like steam punk. I collect stuff and make things out of what I find. That's all I can tell you. I'm not trying to sound like an asshole or anything, but I don't know you well enough to tell you my life story. I'm a private person and I've never brought anyone home before, so I'm finding this very awkward. Bear with me.

"I don't go to bars or hang out socially. I'm more like a hermit. I spend most of my down time in here," she informed him, shrugging her shoulders as she picked up the dishes and went to the sink.

"Whoa, I wasn't trying to step on any toes or sound like I was interrogating you. You saved my bacon, and probably the neighbors as well. You don't know what you did, who you pissed off. That was not some punk kid you ticked off but the mafia's henchmen who came to silence me for good. You put your life in danger by helping me. I have no clue how to thank you for that because now you'll be targeted."

Merrick could see how upset he was becoming, and it made her just about bite her tongue off to keep herself from spewing out everything she was hiding: who she was and what she was doing, but she knew she couldn't do that. A saying sneaked in her mind. In a room full of people and you feel so alone. It made her sad, knowing as long as she was doing this kind of work, she'd never be free to love someone.

To get Stone's mind off Fusion and back on himself, she turned and went to the dryer where she grabbed a towel, washcloth, and a pair of pajama bottoms. "These might be too small for you, but it's all I have." Merrick took the towel and washcloth and disappeared behind a door.

"You're going to be the death of me yet," Merrick yelled, sprinting across the room to steady him. "Are you sure you want to risk a shower?" Her hands automatically reached out, trying to steady him.

"I'm just weak and really sore. You don't have to worry about me. I'm indebted up to my eyeballs to you as it is."

"No!" Her shame made her voice high-pitched. "You don't owe me anything. Don't say that again." Resentment towards herself made her anger evident in her reaction.

If it weren't for her finding the loophole, Gambino would be spending more than one life sentence behind bars. Merrick knew even if she lost her case and he went to jail, Gambino's thugs would have found Stone and killed him and everyone close to him. In her mind, she had prevented his death and the deaths of the people he loved.

The laws, rules or whatever you wanted to call them, were broken, allowing too many criminals to walk the streets, running drugs and creating mayhem in her city. She couldn't let Gambino go to jail. He could and would run his business from behind bars.

"I'm sorry." Merrick looked at the ground instead of his face, slipping her arm around his waist taking his weight. "You don't owe me anything. Okay?"

"Oh no?" Stone's humor surfaced. "Look, I'm standing here bare assed, crippled, and needing your assistance."

She giggled. "Then I'll leave you to it." Merrick's heartbeat thundered in her ears as she backed out of the door, feeling self-conscious. She closed the door and left him to shower.

While he was showering she quickly dressed in a beige, linen corset with brass buttons and a long, dark brown pleated skirt with small chain details, completing her ensemble with dark brown pointy-toed boots. Large brass earrings with glass insets dangled from her ears.

The door opened, catching her attention as Stone came out looking pale as he leaned against the doorjamb. She started towards him to offer her assistance.

"I'm good." He took a step forward, feeling a heavy dizziness overcome him.

Merrick watched him sway and ran to his side. "Okay, big guy, let's get you back into bed. You're trying too hard." Her fingers touched his muscular body as she wrapped her arms around him. Unexpectedly Merrick found herself pressed up against his lean body, and she could not help but drown in his fresh out of the shower scent. Absently she turned her face against his body pretending she was trying to balance him, but in reality she just wanted one last greedy whiff.

She eased Stone onto the bed and handed him the remote. "I'm going out for a while. The rules are as follows: stay here in this room, watch television, read a book, or get online. Just do not get on Facebook or email anyone."

Before she could leave, her cell phone rang. "Hello. This is Hardin. Yes, no." She paused. "I'll have to call you back. Give me about thirty minutes." Another pause. "If your trying to threaten me, don't. Don't you realize to whom you're speaking? Yes, goodbye." She turned and disconnected the call, feeling annoyed.

"Hey, are you okay?" Concern filled his voice. "Who's threatening you? You should call the police and report it."

She ignored his question. "I might be gone a little longer then I first anticipated. I have some business to handle. I'll stop somewhere and pick up some clothes for you. Everything you need is here, and you should try to take a nap or something."

Merrick walked to the door leading to the laundry room. "Remember, don't make any phone calls and don't leave. I left my number by the phone. Oh, and don't answer unless Newton tells you it's me."

"You have two hours to conduct your business, or I'm coming to look for you," Stone replied sounding like a military officer.

"I beg your pardon," she retorted, feeling shocked. "Who do you think you're talking to, some grunt in boot-camp?"

"Forgive me for sounding crass, but there are people out there looking for me, and I suspect searching for you as well. You're not safe out there by yourself."

What he said sparked her memory, so she walked over to her desk and pulled out her steam punk gun. She spun the clip and shoved it into the waistband of her skirt.

For good measure she pocketed extra preloaded cylinders and a few cameo brooches on the outside. With a click of the chamber where the latch was located, the brooches turned into small explosives.

"Thank you for your concern, but I can take care of myself." Fusion jumped up to follow, and Newtown's lights ran across the side of the cycle.

"I'm sorry, Fusion, Newton, I need you here this time. I'll be back shortly." Jynx walked out in a hurry and threw a blouse over her corset, and a blazer to match the long skirt to hide her other outfit before leaving the house.

Four hours later Stone and Fusion heard the door to the basement open. Newton's voice cut across the silence, informing Stone that Merrick was nearly catatonic and stating her vitals.

Chapter 3

"Jynx?" Stone raced to the steps ignoring the pain jolting through his body. When he spotted Jynx slumped against the wall staring off into space and clutching a steering wheel against her chest, Stone paused for a moment stunned for just a spilt second. "What the fuck?" Anger exploded inside him. Stone pushed the anger down; right now the only thing that mattered was to help her. "Jynx?" He tried to draw her out of the shock she obviously was imprisoned behind. He'd seen it many times back in the field when out on tour for the military. It was the body's way of dealing with too much.

When she didn't acknowledge her name or him, Stone listened to his gut instinct. He jumped into military mode and closed the distance between Jynx and himself without realizing he'd moved. His mind calculated the situation, his eyes searching her for any wounds besides the ones on her face.

"I'm just going to check your eyes." Stone spoke clear and calm and at the same time he examined her pupils with a gentle touch to see if they were enlarged. Her pupils did not react and that worried him. Her skin was cool and clammy. Jynx was indeed catatonic. Stone always prided himself on his skills to remember things at a glance. In his line of work, it meant life or death. Puzzled now, he noted her eyes were brown not green, a huge miscalculation on his part.

Jynx offered no resistance as he pulled the steering wheel from her grip. Stone noticed some of her fingernails were broken and bloodied. *What the hell had happened*? he thought, disgusted with himself for allowing her to go out in the first place.

Stone noticed her long brown skirt was singed and ripped. Her corset was ruined, ripped almost off of her body. There was some

kind of material left in tatters around her
neck, from maybe another shirt or blouse she
must have put on over the corset before she
left. And she was barefooted. Her feet were
black, and her big toe was bleeding.

"Everything will be ok, Jynx. You're
safe now with Fusion and Newton watching over
you. Can you see Fusion next to you?" Stone
kept his voice neutral, trying to trigger any
kind of reaction. Deep down he knew she might
be like this for hours.

Inside his anger seethed, building into
a hurricane of retaliation, holding it close
to his chest like a bulletproof vest. At this
moment, Stone was a dangerous killing machine,
but he kept it deep within himself as he
gently reached under her bent knees and
wrapped her in a cocoon of protection, lifting
her against his chest.

"Lock the place down, Newton, and scan
the perimeter. I want to know if anything
moves outside this room," Stone ordered in a
controlled voice not to upset Jynx.

"Accomplished," Newton announced. "Sir,
her pulse is elevated."

Stone stopped at the recliner and
tenderly set her down, kneeling before her
trying to draw her attention. Before he could
fully examine her, Fusion set the first aid
kit at his feet and nosed it closer to Stone's
hand. "Thanks girl," Stone thought Jynx had a
great team with these two machines that were
alive, for the most part because they thought
ahead, almost like a human.

"I'll do what I can for her," Stone
spoke to Fusion keeping a steady pitch of
normalcy.

With the speed of a skilled surgeon he
quickly removed the glass from Jynx's scalp.
Not once did she whimper or cry out in pain.
He went for a bowl of water and washed the
blood from her face, feet and tended to her
bloodied toe before Jynx snapped out of it
into a world of pain.

He left her sitting in the chair while he took the bloodied washcloths to the washing machine and the first aid kit to the bathroom. All the while, he spoke to Jynx quietly in a soothing timbre. As he exited the bathroom, he saw her body visibly start to shake, almost to the point of a seizure. Stone rushed to her side. Unexpectedly she screamed out.

"Jynx," Stone called her name almost yelling himself. Her scream told him she had been afraid. His anger grew.

She mumbled nonsense, her eyes unfocused. The hairs on the back of his neck stood on end. Worry lines etched across his forehead. Patience was not one of his strong suits. He willed her to display any kind of reaction, but Jynx just sat there. Frustrated he stood, glancing around the room.

Since there was nothing else he could do for her, Stone covered her legs with a blanket and settled in to wait. He stood there, looking down at her, wanting to see what he couldn't see. Stone's gut tightened, giving him a warning that's Jynx wasn't as simple as she appeared on the surface. In the military he had relied on his gut instinct. At the moment, though, he couldn't separate if she was dangerous or if she was in danger. All he knew was she had risked her life saving him, and he wasn't going to allow anything to happen to her.

Under normal circumstances Stone could and would have respected her privacy, but now he turned with a mission. With a determined stride he limped around the room, inspecting everything. There was not a document or drawing he didn't read.

"Newton, I know you're loyal to Jynx and her privacy is everything. Right now, I want to protect her, and I need your help. Do you have anything I can go on? Who did this to her?"

"Sorry, sir, but that isn't an option." Stone was upset but more so, he respected

Newton and Fusion for protecting Merrick even though he recognized they were just machines.

Everything he was as a man wanted to shield her, protect her. Hurt the enemy who was not his enemy. The need to keep her safe pushed everything else to the back burner. Nothing was going to happen to her if he had anything to do with it. *When did she burst full speed through a closed door in my heart?* He hadn't even seen it coming. It didn't matter if Newton helped him or not; he had his ways of getting things done.

"Newton, would you turn the television on the local news? Please? Maybe there will be something there that can give me a lead." The TV powered on immediately, and the picture changed to a male reporter. The weather was on, predicting eighty percent thunderstorms tonight.

Another reporter started to give details of Gambino's acquittal. The cameraman showed a close-up of Anthony Gambino. It was that smug, satisfied expression of power he flaunted in front of the people, almost like a warning that he was above the law. Next they showed the defense attorney. She held her head downcast so they couldn't read her face. The attorney stated hardly anything but a quick yes or no and darted into the crowd. He watched the reporters being relentless, and the crowds pushed her, but never once did she retaliate as she escaped to her car. As one cameraman focused on her face, Stone glimpsed the pained look in her eyes, making him doubt his original assessment of her and causing him to question her motives. Maybe Gambino threatened her or worse. It was a real possibility.

"Rumor has it that this attorney could be dirty." A reporter was speaking, drawing Stone's attention.

"Do you know anything about this, Newton?" He couldn't believe he was talking to a motorcycle, but he needed stimulating conversation.

There was a long silence. Stone figured he wasn't going to get any information. He paced back and forth, his mind running full steam ahead.

"You shouldn't go off of hearsay. Influence over the human mind is vast, and wisdom is forgotten within the lines of predictions, instead of facts, sir," Newton announced finally. "I cannot allow you access to her files, but I will gladly be of service to you in any other situation."

Another reporter did a live interview with Judy Velasquez, the owner of Meineke's Muffler shop. Behind the reporter, a dump truck hung from an eighteen-wheeler's tow truck. "The accident happened earlier this evening, located at the Harvey tunnel on the Westbank Expressway." the reporter's voice announced. Wreckage and pieces of debris littered the ground, and a car burned in front of Meineke's parking lot.

"Tell us your account of what happened," the reporter asked Ms. Velasquez.

"Well I don't know when the dump truck parked over in the medium. It was there when I opened my shop this morning, but I thought it was odd because it was facing on-coming traffic. After a while I just forgot about it."

"What happened after that?" The reporter asked curious.

"I was in the office on the phone and the ground under me trembled and all I could hear was brakes squealing, metal crunching, and all sorts of loud noises. I rushed outside and watched the dump truck roll that car smashing it against passing cars, but the truck was only really focused on that one car. It backed up and went for it over and over. Cars were dodging them, but as you can see not everyone escaped. There was an explosion and we were thrown to the ground."

"I know this had to be so horrendous for you to witness." The reporter continued.

"A woman was thrown from a car right before it exploded. I think she might be dead. Two other people died in front of my shop today. I can't deal with this. My employee's are upset and I've sent everyone home, I'm shutting it down for today. When everyone is done I'm out of here."

"Thank you, Judy Valasquez, for your report of what has shaken all of us in this bizarre accident."

"Man, if you fucking think that was an accident." Judy shook her head in denial and walked away, Oblivious to the camera and anyone watching. She must have thought them idiots because she didn't even finish what she was trying to say.

The reporter turned towards the camera. "All that's left of what has been identified now as defense attorney Merrick Hardin's car is scrap metal," the reported stated.

"When police and paramedics arrived on the scene, both drivers were missing from their vehicles. Suspicion falls on the crime lord, Anthony Gambino. Attorney Hardin represented him recently on his current charges," the reporter finished.

Stone caught a glimpse of the wreckage and the remains of the car and looked at Jynx who slept in the recliner. He sat up straight. "Those bastards who killed the senator's wife were trying to kill them all." Rage curled through him. Now he knew he must have threatened the attorney who defended him. It was all in her eyes. That bastard is trying to kill him, the attorney and accidentally almost killed Jynx. Something was missing, but he couldn't put his finger on it.

"Damn. I could use my briefcase." The words were blurted out in frustration. Stone needed to secure the area and do some recon. He needed the blueprints of their hideout. Some of his equipment was in his case that he had left behind. He'd have to find a way to handle this without it. The case would only make things easier and take less effort.

Stone could make a phone call. No questions would be asked. He had recruited and trained the members of his team himself. They were the only ones he trusted with his life. His eyes went to Jynx curled up in the chair sleeping. She seemed so fragile and feminine, but he knew she was iron and tough when she needed to be. Stone liked that about her.

Something was not sitting right with Stone. All his senses went on full alert. Jynx was hurt and had been carrying a steering wheel. The news reported the attorney's car had been involved in the wreckage. He wanted to laugh. Jynx didn't dress or look like any attorney he'd ever seen.

On the other hand, why would a petite woman have a basement secured so well the military couldn't get in without her knowing it? His little Jynx had some secrets. What did he really know about her anyway? Stone shrugged off the thought. He didn't really care. She had saved his ass, and he was holed up in her basement, hidden from the world under her protection.

Now it was his turn to return the favor. He would make sure whatever had happened to Jynx while she had been out would not happen again. He walked over to the bed. Suddenly it occurred to him she had received a phone call earlier, and whoever it had been had threatened her. He needed to find her phone.

Jynx was out for at least four hours. He smiled. She wasn't going to be too happy when she found out he'd given her Excedrin P.M's. He'd take a short nap to rejuvenate and gain some energy.

* * *

The sound of Newton's alarm jerked Jynx awake and she burst from her chair at a dead run to the computer. She noticed Stone did the same thing. The three screens showed ten men wearing black, penetrating the boundaries of her property. She was holding her head, while watching the camera.

A man jumped the fence at the back gate and fell into the hedges. He screamed into the night as a trap with huge steel thorns stopped him cold.

"Impressive," Stone said.

Jynx nodded, her attention on the monitor.

Jynx felt Stone's body lean towards her, watching her and the monitors. "Thank you for watching over me while I was having an overload." She felt more than a little humiliated. She considered herself a warrior, a fighter, and not some weak-minded female. Since she had rescued him, her body didn't feel like her own. Like right now, the heat from him made her feel things. She bit her lip hard to make herself stop from making a sound. Her eyes closed for a split second to regain control over her aroused body. She needed to focus on the situation outside, not on him.

"No problem, but you should let me take care of this. You have been through a lot. I can't explain what I'm capable of doing, but trust me when I say I can do this," Stone stated.

She could sense his rage. "Don't think for a moment I'm going to let you have all the fun," her voice trembled slightly. She was a little shocked by her reaction to him. "We'll wait for them to get closer." She touched his arm, trying to soothe his male ego of his attempt at protection.

"Mistress, I deployed Fusion to her position. She awaits her orders." Jynx took the news in stride and shoved a pair of military noise-canceling headphones at Stone. "Put these on." She adjusted hers quickly, as she watched the screen. "On my mark," she ordered Newton firmly. She leaned over and automatically adjusted Stone's headphones so he wouldn't be affected. Jynx watched how his eyes stared into hers. It sent shivers down her spine.

"Brace yourself. I've only tested this once." Jynx smiled mischievously up at Stone.

She felt the high adrenaline rush over her. "This is so exciting," Jynx laughed catching Stone's surprised expression as she watched the screen.

She watched Fusion move to the middle of the yard. Her nerves gathered in the pit of her stomach. Stone stood next to her, waiting. "On my count: three, two, one." The order was engaged. Fusion roared and a small device flew from her mouth and exploded.

The small bushes in the yard uprooted and the ground itself shook suddenly. The house moaned from the electromagnetic pulse waves. The ground under their feet rippled with the current of energy. Furniture moved and dishes fell. Chaos broke out around Jynx. "Oh, shit!" she screeched loudly, caught by surprise as she lost her balance.

Jynx slammed into Stone and as they were going down his arms wrapped around her tightly and his body shifted quickly, pushing her body above his so that he would hit the floor and not her. Jynx's elbow struck his ribs, and she heard the rush of air from the unexpected jab, but his grip never wavered as he cushioned her soft curves.

Jynx felt his arousal as her body was cradled against his jeans. The urge to push her bottom against him was almost more than she could bear. Her eyes shut as her senses wanted to feel more of him. He was so strong, his body perfect. With the force of her own desires she found her bottom rubbing against the hardness of his erection. She heard his intake of breath and secretly she smiled. "I'm sorry! I couldn't help it that my elbow caught you." She wasn't an attorney for nothing. Jynx's voice came out a little hoarse, but she had to think on her feet in the courtroom. She hoped the simple statement might make him believe it was an accident and not her hormones going all over the place.

When everything settled, she found herself lying on the ground mourning the loss of his body no longer touching hers. What was

with her! Jynx had been around people before,
and none of them had affected her in any way.
Her hormones almost always stayed dormant.
With Stone, she found herself more than once
imagining herself doing things she only
thought happened in romance books.

Her face flamed knowing the answer; she
craved his touch more and more. She watched
him as he stood over her staring into her
soul, and his expression in itself was
unreadable. Jynx couldn't look away, caught up
in the way he was looking at her. She felt it
deep inside and shivered as he reached down
and practically lifted her to her feet. A
little "O" escaped in surprise.

"Who are you, lady? Where did you get an
EMP?" he asked.

Without answering she smiled. "I'm full
of surprises." It was all she could say, all
she could tell him. Jynx couldn't allow
herself the luxury of lowering her guard.

Jynx noticed how he turned away,
shutting her out. She realized he wanted her
to trust him, but how could she really. He
didn't know who she really was and when he
found out, everything would change. She would
once again be alone. Just the thought of that
made her feel empty. It seemed to her as he
walked stiffly to the computer table to see
the monitors that maybe she should give him
some space. When she headed toward the stairs,
Jynx didn't even see him move, but all of a
sudden he was crowding her personal space.

"You can't go upstairs yet. It isn't
safe," Stone commanded.

Jynx welcomed the anger as she pointedly
gave him the evil eye, a look she used in the
courtroom at times. It worked more times than
it didn't.

"I realize you're not the average
woman," Stone said.

But Jynx needed to check things out.
This was her house. It was her duty to see
things through even though he didn't
understand.

She watched him throw his hands up, showing he was backing off at her irritated expression. She wanted to smile, but that would ruin the look that she was trying to portray.

"Before we go barging upstairs, let's look over the house using Newton's cameras or Fusion? We don't need any surprises."

"We? I keep hearing the word 'we'. I hate to inform you, but you're under my protection. Someone is trying to kill you." The annoyance came out before she could stop it. Jynx turned toward the sound of Newton's voice. "Sorry, mistress, but Fusion is down."

Jynx ducked around Stone and ran towards the stairs, screaming for Newton to turn off the security to the door. She didn't slow down, bursting into the laundry room. The feeling of panic filled her every fiber. Fusion had never been down before. She couldn't lose her! They were a team, more so her family. Her mind went off the deep end, thinking the unthinkable. The outer door wouldn't budge at all. She pushed and shoved against the entrance to the kitchen. Frustrated, Jynx beat on the door with her fists. Tears burned behind her eyes threatening to roll down her cheeks.

Fusion was her baby. She slept with her, and she was alive in most standards. The word "down" repeated itself, making her head pound in a sudden headache. She couldn't handle it. Too much had happened lately. She wondered if this was a sign. Hot tears rolled down her cheeks as she pushed at the door. The worst part of it was Jynx wasn't sure if she could fix Fusion.

She panicked as found herself airborne. Before she could mutter a word, Stone leaned back and kicked the door. At the sound of splintering wood giving way, Merrick shoved past him at a dead run. She surveyed the damage to her home without a blink of the eye. Merrick didn't give a damn about the house. Her paced slowed, and she noticed that one of barstools had blocked the door, which had prevented her from opening it.

She sensed Stone on her heels. When she grabbed the handle of the door leading outside, his arm snaked around her waist, pulling her abruptly against his body and stopping any further movement.

"You're not thinking clearly. You can't go bursting out there not knowing if anyone is out there waiting to kill you," Stone hissed in her ear.

"Get behind me and if I move, you better be my second skin, you understand? Or you can stay behind, and I'll go get Fusion."

Jynx moved to a heavy potted plant against the wall, put her hand in the dirt, and pulled out a ziplock baggy containing a pistol, a silencer, and a small object she slipped into her pocket. She turned to Stone after she threw the bag on the ground, and quickly started to twist the silencer in place. "I understand."

"Ready?" he asked.

"Yes, let's go. You're wasting time." She watched Stone open the door a crack and study the area. He moved an inch, Jynx was on him, hugging his body with hers.

She gripped the back waistband of his pants, trying to see over him, but he wouldn't budge. Every fiber wanted to push him out the way. What he said made sense; they needed to be careful in case of an ambush. Someone was trying to kill her and him, and deep down Jynx knew it was the same person.

Stone stopped suddenly and Jynx bumped into him.

"Why are you stopping?" Jynx hissed.

"Go back inside and let me go find Fusion."

"What is it? What's the matter?" Merrick tried to see around him. "Let me by." Desperately she shoved him to move out of the way, but he was like a brick wall.

"Trust me. You don't want to see her like this."

It was what he said, the look in his eyes. She knew in her gut he had seen Fusion out there.

"Get out of the way and let me see! Damn you!" Dread filled her knowing what was out there wasn't good. Hot angry tears threatened to escape. "Either you move out of my way," she hissed, "or you will regret it."

"Let me go get her for you."

"Move!" she screamed and shoved at his rock hard chest. "You're wasting valuable time. If you're going to help me save Fusion, let's go now!"

She didn't wait but shoved him enough that as soon as she could fit she burst from the house.

Stone grabbed her by the arm, stopping her in her tracks. "Please don't, you can put her back together."

Jynx heard what he said. "The thing is I don't know if I can fix her!" The shrill statement broke the barrier of Jynx's restraint and she cried in earnest.

Heavy drops of rain started slowly, then a sudden torrent of rain drenched everything. Just as suddenly, Stone's words slammed into her brain. "What do you mean, I can put her back together?" Jynx tugged and struggled against his grip. "Let me go!" With a sudden jerk she slipped under his arm, free. Jynx paused, not sure where to look for Fusion.

Her dreads weighed down with rainwater, and her clothes were instantly soaked. Jynx raised her hand to stop the flow of water running down her face so she could search the yard until she spotted Fusion. Her piercing scream of denial pushed her into action. Jynx raced across the yard and her body collapsed, sliding to a stop next to Fusion whose body lay in pieces.

"No!" The denial rushed from her throat. Jynx picked up Fusion's head and laid it in her lap. Tears streamed down her face, her body rocked back and forth in the rain. She felt so much anger. "You're all dead!" she screamed into the sky, so loudly it made her voice hoarse.

An arm grabbed her shoulder hard and yanked her flat to the ground in a tumble of arms and legs, and she ended up with an unidentified person on top of her. Somehow she lost her grip on her gun and dropped it. The assailant held her arms above her head, pinning her to the ground. Before she could react she saw Stone fighting off an attacker only a few feet from her. It was an ambush. *This is not happening, these fuckers are going to die!* Jynx locked her legs around his neck and twisted, straining every muscle as she rolled with the masked man until she was on top.

Her assailant was strong with a medium built but that didn't scare Jynx. She reached into her pocket and pulled out small device and shoved it in the attacker's mouth while she struggled with him, holding her hand tightly over his mouth until he swallowed.

Jynx jumped off, watching the stunned look on his face when she released him. She looked him in the eye and waited as she counted down silently, watching his features twist in pain. She turned away, and located her gun on the ground, picked it up, and walked away.

The explosion, when it came, sent blood and gore in every direction. There wasn't much left except for what she was wearing. Bits and pieces were tangled in her hair and splatted up her back. Jynx just kept walking.

Another person dressed in black came out of nowhere, and Jynx shot him dead in the heart without any compassion. They killed a member of her family and all she felt was anger and hate. Jynx was tired of playing games.

As far she as was concerned they all could die. The problem wasn't with Fusion's body parts she could replace any of the missing pieces. What scared her was what made Fusion real. To Jynx, it was like having a death in the family. She felt defeated as she went to her knees in front of what was left of Fusion. Huge broken sobs consumed her.

She watched Stone squat down and start gathering up the separated pieces. Jynx stood up with the front part of Fusion and followed behind him inside to her worktable.

"Lock us down, Newton," Jynx demanded in a commanding attitude, which required immediate compliance as her mind rushed ahead to what she needed to begin.

Jynx's one-track mind concentrated on prepping her equipment as she walked to the dryer and started peeling off her wet clothes. She stood nude, wiping off the blood and gore and rainwater from her body with a towel, mechanically going through the steps. Her hands kept wiping at the same spot trying to get rid of the gore of the assailant. *Get off me, damn you.*

The clearing of Stone's throat yanked Merrick's thoughts back to the present, and she stared into his eyes across the room. Her eyes traveled down his body and paused at the bulge in his jeans. She looked up fast. Her face flamed as she watched him watching her.

"I wasn't," she paused her eyes never wavering from his. "I am not used to," pausing again. "I'm sorry."

She turned and quickly wiggled into in a long skirt and long sleeved t-shirt with a picture of a steam punk girl holding a gun.

"Love the tattoos." His voice came out a little hoarse.

"Thank you." Merrick strode over to the workbench and turned on the overhead light where Fusion lay on the table.

"Mistress, from my analysis Fusion is missing a bolt and a medium sized metallic gear for fastening her hip in place." Before she could move, Stone placed the missing pieces on the table.

She looked up at him, her eyes stared straight into his, but Stone realized Jynx really didn't see him. By her posture and the determined set of her jaw, she was totally focused on Fusion. Impatience showed in her movements as her hands lifted her dreads and tied them behind her head.

"I'm ready to begin, Newton," Jynx's voice wavered, revealing her uncertainty. The normal routine of things included all three of them. When she had created Fusion and Newton it was a fluke, a miracle had happened. Ever since then, she tinkered with things, but she never succeeded with any other creations like she had with the two of them and the goggles. She walked around her table and turned on her machines which were robots that gave her an extra set of hands. She had gotten the idea from car dealerships and how they put cars together with machines instead of using people. She just made hers more personal, small.

Tonight would be different. Somewhere deep inside of herself Jynx knew she had to think positive and believe. She touched a screwdriver with a finger. Her hand moved on to the wrench. Her gaze went to Fusion's face, and tears burned down her cheeks. Angrily she wiped them away with the back of her sleeve as rage consumed her every thought with the idea of revenge.

"Mistress, please take a step back," Newton addressed her formally and with respect. "All the pieces are collected and assembled on the table to reassemble Fusion. You have done everything. Now please remove yourself."

Jynx didn't understand why she was asked to move, but she did so stumbling awkwardly, feeling like her world had just fallen apart. She knew Newton would never jeopardize Fusion's existence.

"The Three Musketeers are eternal," Newton's words rang out through the basement. Feeling confused Jynx glanced at Stone. "What are you doing, Newton?" The question burst from Jynx's lips as she turned to face the cycle.

"Wait. Look!" Stone excitement cut whatever Newton's reply might have been.

A three dimensional hologram penetrated the room from within Newton's cycle to hover over the worktable.

She felt the table shake as one of the machines moved its arm out to begin its repairs. Merrick jerked around at the same moment as Stone's outburst. There was a loud popping noise, and white sparks of light jumped from the mechanical arm holding a piece of equipment to a section of Fusion's body to the dislocated pieces, soldering them back together with great care.

A prototype robot moved with direction and began to put the pieces of Fusion together. Merrick had created the machine to help her when she needed another person. She never relied on people, so she had created her own crew. The robot pulled the wires across the workbench, attaching the wires to various body parts. It rattled noisily in search of the other side and fused pieces together. Gears turned in place, and screws bolted down tightly with the help of the machine working diligently, changing smoothly from screwdrivers to wrenches. Within minutes Fusion's body was complete once again.

"I would have never thought of such a miracle." Stone moved to the side of the table next to Jynx.

Jynx couldn't breathe as she stood in shock, watching. She knew she could put the body back together. That wasn't the problem. What made Fusion real was what mattered most. Her hand grabbed Stone, jerking him back to her side. "Wait," she whispered desperately, hoping against the odds. She tried to read the hologram, realizing it wasn't her notes or anything she had put together. This was not her work but from her machines. *How is that possible?*

Chapter 4

"All is complete." Newton assessed the progress of Fusion's repairs on the table. The hologram dissolved into nothingness. After what seemed forever, Fusion's eyes opened. She raised her head and looked at Jynx and her tail thumped against the table in excitement.

Jynx threw her arms around Fusion's neck, laughing through happy tears. "Oh girl, I thought I lost you," she murmured, burying her head against the hard shell of Fusion's cat face.

She rose up. "Thank you, Newton. I owe you everything. You two are my family. I would be so lost without you. Look, my hands are shaking.

"What about the hologram, Newton? It's not my work." Questions pumped inside Jynx's mind, running full force as she tried to process what had happened.

"Fusion and I have worked together and created a program as a fail safe system, just in case something ever happened to either one of us," Newton replied. "We will always remain at your side, Mistress."

"I don't know what to say except I love you both. You're my children and the reason I come home at night." Jynx glanced at Stone. Feeling sentimental, she turned away to hide her face. No one ever saw her like this, all mushy and stuff, and within hours of his hiding out at her house, he'd become so involved in her life. She was more than a little afraid once he knew the truth about her, he'd hate her for sure.

She moved to step away from him, but his arm stopped her.

"What happened just now? You looked sad for a moment."

"It's nothing. All is good. Fusion is back," Jynx quickly reassured him, feeling guilty.

"Do you realize how talented you are and what you have here? No wonder you keep

48

this place locked down. We have to keep them safe."

"Fusion is fully functional, and her memories have been restored," Newton announced, sounding joyous himself.

"What you have here," Stone continued, "is a gold mine, something that needs to be protected above all else. I wish I'd had been able to keep my briefcase close. I have money, guns and a few extra toys that could give us help. I could help out."

Fusion bounced off the table. "Wait Fusion, don't you think you should rest?" Jynx worried, unsure if her baby should be moving around. Her soldering might not be fully dried.

Newton piped in. "She'll be right back."

"Do you think it's safe for her to be moving around? Newton?"

"She's fully functional," Newton reported.

Before Jynx could argue Fusion was back with a briefcase in her mouth.

"What the hell!" Stone said in surprise.

"Well it looks like you have your briefcase." Jynx smiled and reached down to hug Fusion. "You're amazing." She whispered.

"Thank you, girl. I never leave home without it. Thanks to you, now I'm complete."

The next thing Jynx knew Stone grabbed her around the waist and lifted her from the ground, swinging her in a circle. Her squeal of surprise was as unexpected as being swung around in his arms.

She wrapped her arms around his neck, and her fingers found his short hair. From the first moment she'd seen him, she had been painfully attracted to him. Jynx ran her fingers through his military hair cut. He was so handsome sometimes while in court she had found it difficult to look at him. Now having him here in her home, she burned for his touch. Jynx's heart pounded harder, faster. A fire burned in her belly. Inexperienced as she was, all she knew was she craved more.

She slid intimately against his chest, causing her skirt to hike up and allowing her to wrap her legs around his waist. Jynx placed her hands on each side of his face to hold him in place and touched her lips to his tentatively at first waiting for his reaction. When he kissed her back, her hands gripped him tighter with the need to be even closer. Under the pressure of his kiss she opened her mouth for him. Their tongues touched and played together in sweet glory. All her emotions crashed, filling Jynx with a yearning only he could extinguish.

The contact was not enough. With every second that passed, her body burned for more. She found herself under his control as he coached her with his mouth, fueling her desires.

She was crushed against his chest as she realized her nipples became very sensitive to the touch of his body. Little sparks of awareness zinged down to her toes. Then her hair was released, encasing them in a cloud of her dreads.

Her hands were touching Stone everywhere. The warmth of his body made her want more. The taste of him made her moan into his mouth. Lost in the hunger of need she had no idea when they moved, but the next thing she realized through the haze of desire was that Stone cleared off the kitchen table in one swipe. The sound of shattering dishes hitting the floor barely registered in her mind, but Jynx didn't care; she wanted whatever he was offering.

The table was cold to her naked bottom and the sudden cool air hit her nipples when he pulled her t-shirt over her head.

She needed to be closer to him, skin to skin. The need burning in her couldn't be satisfied. *Should I tell him I am a virgin?* The thought anxiously entered her mind and it made her pause. This seemed right. The way he made her feel only made her want more. Jynx wasn't about to go into the why nots. She'd

have plenty of time to berate herself later,
and deep down she had already started because
she wasn't stopping this from happening in the
first place. She should stop him, stop this
from happening, but she realized she wasn't
going to.

"What? What's wrong?" Stone questioned.

When she looked into his eyes she
noticed the worry. "Nothing, nothing at all."
To prove to herself she was going to do this
with Stone, she reached for him, pulling his
lips closer to hers, and nibbled on his bottom
lip.

His fingers were rough and calloused,
and the feel of them on her body sent shivers
straight to the heart of her desire. She was
damp, ready and aching for what he would do
with her body. Jynx tried to picture it in her
head to prepare herself, but she only had
movies to relate to. She was lost in thought
when Stone ran his tongue over one of her
nipples and his teeth closed over it and
pulled. Jynx almost leaped off the table. On
their own her fingers pulled his face closer
to her body as she squirmed to get closer to
him.

She jerked when Stone pushed her legs
apart and touched her where her body ached the
most severely. The hoarse moan pushed past her
lips, Jynx's eyes shut and her head felt heavy
as it rolled back. The new sensations erupted
throughout her body and she became lost in the
euphoria that consumed her senses. The more he
touched her the more her out control body
raised up against his fingers for more. Jynx
felt wanton, and giddy and she poured herself
into every sensation knowing deep down she
found paradise.

Jynx watched from under her lashes how
he moved. How strong he was but gentle with
her. With both hands Stone reached up to the
waistband of her skirt and with a sudden jerk
it was around her ankles and disappeared. Jynx
didn't protest but now she was totally nude
and modesty creeped causing a blush to spread

over her body. No man has ever seen her naked before. It was another first. Stone didn't seem to notice she hesitated slightly or the sudden feeling of being unsure which was a good thing, maybe. She wasn't positive.

"Beautiful!" He whispered.

Silently tears burned behind her eyes. *He called her beautiful. Being the outcast of the city a compliment was rarely given freely. It was another first. She held it close to her heart, savoring the feeling. The only person called her things like that was her mom and how often was that having to keep her hidden.*

He made her feel beautiful, wanted by someone. She shivered when his hot breath tickled her skin as he trailed fleeting kisses down her body and leaving little bite marks causing undignified reactions. Jynx body didn't seem to belong to herself as her hips shifted upwards for more of his attentions.

"Oh!" she gushed in surprise as he grabbed both ankles and raised them high into the air and spread wide. Her hands flew to her face to cover her eyes in embarrassment. She found herself so open, vulnerable it made her eyes squeeze shut tight. His attention was focused between her legs. Deep inside her conscious raised his ugly head telling her to pull away. Before she could react Stone went down on his knees.

His lips touched her inner thigh kissing her. It was like hitting a nerve and when she felt his teeth against her skin. She wasn't thinking about pulling away anymore. A finger touched her sex softly rubbing. Her hips bucked from the contact and she moaned loudly. All cohered thoughts fled. The only thing that mattered was Stone.

When his hot tongue licked her in the place that raged and suckled close around her womanhood. "Please!" She begged.

Was that her? Begging? She knew the voice, someplace where sane and normal dwelled, but she didn't sound like herself. Her voice was throaty, deep. She moaned, her head thrashed side to side as her hips came off the table. "Stone." His name was a hoarse whisper.

He raised his head and hovered over her sex. Jynx opened her eyes and looked between her legs until their eyes locked. Memorized she couldn't look away as she watched Stone lean forward and rubbed his day old stubble against her sex. It sent sparks of fire through her body. Jynx's hands reached out and fisted her fingers into his hair pushing his face into her sex. "Please!" Her hips moved on their own accord against the friction. The more she rubbed the more intense the throbbing became and it was the ultimate feeling.

On cue, Stone's hot tongue licked her pussy lips leaving a trail of kisses and little bites. She whimpered in frustration at his teasing. When he grabbed her legs and held them apart she held her breathe.

Her body jerked when his tongue pushed past the lips of her womanhood into the secret closure. His breath was warm when he drove his tongue deep inside. Jynx squealed loudly.

Her body pushed her sex into his face. His finger went inside her. Her hips met him with a urgent force.

Her body stiffened, lights flashed behind her eyes as her first orgasm hit, rippling through her body like a huge tidal wave. After the sparks receded Jynx sat up, reached behind his neck pulling herself closer, and kissed him, driving her tongue into his mouth. In between kissing him and the need to get closer, she tugged on his shirt, trying to push it up and over his head. He ended up helping her take it off and threw it behind him.

While he pulled his shirt off, she unbuttoned his jeans in record time, pulling on the zipper. Her hand went to the waistband and started to push them down. Jynx felt when his hands went to each side and shoved the jeans down his legs being impatient. She hid a smile at this actions, realizing he wanted her just as much.

Before Stone could take charge of their next step, Jynx looked into his eyes bravely grasped his erection in her hand. She never broke eye contact as she covered him with her hot mouth and captured him. She heard him moan and that edge her on with confidence. Sliding her tongue over his manhood she marveled at his reaction. The sense of power she had to make him react to her was enthralling.

She moved one hand over his erection, gripping his balls, pulling on them, feeding her mouth at the same time with his hardness. His harsh cries and the feel of his body trembling with desire fed her pleasure, arousing her for more.

With a sigh of impatience Stone removed her grip on him and kissed her possessively full of passion. Jynx returned the kiss with the same fervor until she sensed he was pushing her backwards to make her lie back on the table. Her dreads covered her eyes preventing her from seeing him.

He urged her to the edge of the table and Jynx scooted, gripping her ankles he spread her legs wide to accept his body between her legs. Jynx couldn't look away as he rubbed his erection back and forth against her sex. In the back of her mind she was nervous. She didn't know what to expect, but the pleasure again took control. She felt him pushing pressure at her opening and she craved more. Hesitantly she push against him, waiting. It was driving her beyond insane. Her head thrashed from side to side.

"Please," She begged him, aching inside. Jynx had never experienced anything so erotic in her life. The secrets in her life flashed in her mind for a split second, but she didn't ever want this to end. She realized she loved him or she wouldn't have allowed him to become this close to her. Deep down there was a part of her that realized she wanted him since the first time she seen him in court. Somehow she had to make this right. At the moment she couldn't stop herself if she wanted to, and she didn't want to.

When his movements changed it drew her attention back to him as his erection pressed against the folds of her womanhood. It was so tight she felt the sparks of fire burning with just the weight set against her virgin body.

Jynx pushed against him in one brave move and impaled herself. She screamed in pain and locked her legs around his body so neither one of them could move. She was panting trying to breath through the fire.

"Sweet Gezus!"

Silent tears rolled down her face. Now the embarrassment part hit and she covered her eyes with her hands.

"You're a virgin! Sweet Gezus Jynx. If I would have known this would have gone totally differently."

"It's my fault. I'm sorry. She mumbled under her breath.

"I'm not going to move. Wait for your body to get use to mine and we'll go from there. You're in control of what happens now."

The muscles in her legs trembled from the force of how she wrapped them around his body so he couldn't move. Self-protection. After a few minutes her body ease and when the pain lessened. She allowed her legs to move.

She noticed sweat broke out on his forehead and down his arms. He was as good as his word. He hasn't moved a muscle. The control over his body was a lesson she needed to apply to herself. When he bit. That was such a turn on because she realized she was affecting him.

"Try to breathe through the pain. I know it's hard, but try to relax your muscles. "Breath in and out through your mouth. Move whenever your ready."

She panted in short puffs of air, feeling awkward at first. Her hands reduced their death grip on the table. Her whole body was so sensitive to his slightest touch. She felt him inside her full, complete in a way she had never imagined. There was a whirlwind of sensations as she moved her hips, and behind her closed eyes, sparks flew like the fourth of July. Her body ached with a fierce need, but she moved cautiously, waiting for the pain. He was so big. He filled her completely; it was like coming home. Her body had waited all this time for him. Her eyes connected with his, seeing desire in his eyes and strain around his mouth.

Lifting her hips, she pushed him deeper, feeling his body fill her. The fierce expression of pleasure she saw cross his face urged her on. Slowly, cautiously, Jynx repeated the action. Stone started to move adding to her pleasure.

After awhile her body demanded more. The friction of her movements caused a firestorm in her blood. Without knowing why, the feel of him inside her urged her to move a little faster, harder until she found herself practically slamming her body against his in a fevered momentum until her body jerked, spasmed, She screamed.

Her fingers dug into his skin to hang on while Stone kept pace, and he groaned deeply, the sound drawing her attention to his face. She watched as he threw his head back as he too climaxed. Ripples of a second orgasm hit her, and she moved with fevered pleasure. Every few seconds her whole body jerked hard in gratification. All went still, spent, except the aftereffects of small spasm.

Jynx found his lips on hers, kissing her soft, slow and she returned the sweet kisses in the same fashion, so caught up in emotions she wasn't yet able to express with words. She closed her eyes and curled into a ball. His arms reached under her body and lifted her. Jynx snuggled into his large frame. The next thing she knew Stone laid her on the bed and moved in next to her, pulling the sheet over them.

She must have dozed off, Jynx wasn't
sure, but when she opened her eyes and looked
around, the lights were dimmed to almost pitch
black, giving the basement a romantic feel.
Until now she hadn't noticed there was cello
music playing. More than a little embarrassed
she squirmed to sit up, the sheet falling to
her waist.

What did I just do? Jynx thought to
herself as she covered her face with her
hands. *How stupid could I be*? She had let her
guard down and allowed her attraction to
overrule her better judgment. She glanced down
to see he was still sleeping. With great care
not to disturb Stone, she edged out of bed.
She just made things more difficult. He knew
her as a lie, not the person who was the
attorney who had put his life in danger. She
remembered his face when he was leaving the
courtroom. He had been disappointed, angry.

Quiet as a mouse Jynx picked up her
clothes and tiptoed to a secret door leading
to an underground passage. When she turned,
Fusion was standing at her side. She dressed
quickly, and without a word she opened the
door, giving Fusion room to pass. With a click
and lock, she moved through the passageway.
She didn't feel like talking or explaining
because in her mind there wasn't really
anything she could say.

It was getting close to morning and she
needed to clear her head. She grabbed the keys
from the key holder against the wall of her
garage. The keys for her candied apple red
1962 Vintage Volkswagen double cab pickup
truck with the slit front windshield and spoke
rim tires. The truck was one of her favorites
to drive when she needed to reflect on her day
because the old VW had class and personality
all its own. She opened the back door and
Fusion jumped inside. Jynx opened her door and
sat on the cool bench seat. Before she pulled
off she pulled out her regular cell phone and
dialed a number.

"Good Morning Susan." Jynx paused.

"Morning Miss Jynx. It's nice to hear from you. How may I help you?" The voice inquired.

"I need housekeeping for six rooms. Please. I'm not at home but the usual will be paid.

"It's not a problem. Do you want the normal or deep cleaning?" Said the voice.

"I prefer the deep. Can the girls show up as soon as possible?

"That will cost extra." The voice related with a sweet girlie tone.

"Yes, not a problem. You know where to reach me if there is a issue. Thank you." Jnyx hung up. *When Stone wakes up looking for dead bodies, there won't be a trace of evidence. The girls detail to the extreme.*

Now that that issue has been taken care of, she turned the key to her baby and listened, as she purred to life. She clicked the remote opener to the garage door. It opened quietly on its hinges. Every part of her life demanded she'd use safety precautions. If she needed a quick getaway, she couldn't afford the garage to squeak and moan. Keeping her equipment fine-tuned was imperative.

It was still pretty dark as Jynx pulled onto St. Charles Street. A few cars moved casually through morning traffic as it was a workday for most. Gradually as time passed, the colors of daylight started to change the skyline. Canal Street had its usual traffic as she turned on Decatur Street. When she was upset, she automatically treated herself to Café du Monde for some beignets and coffee.

She drove her truck in a parking lot and paid ten dollars for the secured location. Fusion stayed behind as she got out. Jynx needed some quiet time to make a new plan.

There was the usual long line before you could place your order, but it moved at a steady pace. Conversation with some of the others made the wait seem not so bad. Finally, she placed her order and quickly she paid for her purchase before moving out of line. "Have a great day." Jynx expressed to the people behind her in line, waving as she left.

She walked the block to reach the levee and sat on an empty bench close to the river's edge, folding her legs up against her chest. She watched the river's traffic move through the water. The smell of the water, the way it constantly moved, relaxed her. A jogger passed by with headphones without paying her a second thought.

Back to the problem, she thought with dismay. It was just plain stupid, stupid, stupid on her part. She wanted to kick herself, physically as much as mentally. Jynx was so confused because for the first time she really was attracted to someone with a brain.

It wasn't like they could be together. Her life was too complicated, too extreme, and he was military. Once her secret was out, he would hate her. A hard knot rolled in her belly at the thought of his disapproval. The disappointment on his face or the mistrust it would just end her. Jynx could almost taste the bile. He was the kind of man that wouldn't wait around for her to explain. And if she did, would he be open-minded? Jynx didn't think so. Her fate had been set long ago when she decided how she was going to clean up her city. The promise was made to her deceased father, and she kept her promises, not some broken promise made from a Politician.

So with that in mind, she straightened her spine, needing the determination to face her fears. She didn't know how to face him, but she wasn't sorry. How could she be? She was sorry Gambino had gunned him down. She should have been there sooner, but the reporters coupled with the graffiti on her car had been a hard day.

Jynx felt the tears burn behind her eyes. She let them roll down her cheeks for a moment, resigned to the rare show of weakness. For once, just this one time, she wished things could be different. She wanted someone

to love her. Really love her, stand in front
her for a change. Was that a crazy request?
Maybe for her it was, but it didn't' stop her
from wishing.

It had been over five years since she
had seen her mom. It was too dangerous to
visit, not when the top criminals in the city
wanted to get their hands on her, to control
her, to make her their puppet. For just an
instant she imagined being loved, living a
normal life. Well, not completely normal, but
to be herself. Angrily she brushed the tears

away with the back of her hand. Something's
were just not meant to be.

Jynx stood, but a wave of intense
loneliness swamped her, almost to the point of
more tears. "Ugh!" she screeched. How could
she win, when her mind was telling her one
thing and her heart something else?

The air left her in a rush as she was
slammed to ground. Excruciating pain shot
through her skull, and she saw stars. Before
she could recover, the assailant punched her
in the face, busting her lip. From the
position she was in, she raised her knee fast
and hard, hitting him in the groin. She
entangled her leg with his and rolled him
until she was the one of top. Quickly she
moved her body and pinned him, applying
pressure until the man started to screech in
earnest.

"You should start talking if you don't
want a broken arm," Jynx hissed in his ear
while she used her hips on against the ground
to keep him pinned. "I bet you weren't
expecting this, were you, a woman fighting
back. How original."

Before she could get an answer out of
him, someone grabbed her violently from behind
and dragged her off. She tried to roll but the
person holding her shifted so he held her by
the neck. She tangled her leg with his and
pushed back forcing both of them to fall
backwards.

Jynx twisted her body just enough to elbow him hard in his ribs. She caught a glimpse of her red Volkswagen pickup truck bouncing across the uneven ground. "Fusion!" She screamed. The next thing she knew Fusion was attacking. Two of the men were caught off guard, screaming with pain as her metal jaguar sank her small razor sharp teeth into her attackers, tearing flesh. A gunshot echoed loudly making her ears ring. A man fell to the ground close to her head. Jynx noticed a dart sticking out of his chest.

The sound of a motorbike approaching made Jynx turn her head. Newton was tearing up the distance with Stone on him. Anger consumed his features. Jynx could tell Stone had murder in his eyes. Before Newton could stop, Jynx watched Stone jump off at a dead run.

The person who held her around the neck now placed a knife to her throat. He was choking her with his death grip as he jerked her against his chest, facing Stone. Jynx tried to stay calm when she felt the knife make a cut.

"Let her go, and we'll just call it a day." Stone held his arms out wide to show he meant it.

"I'm not buying that load of shit. You must think I'm a fool. I wasn't born yesterday. As soon as I let the little lady go, you'll be on me like red beans on rice," the man who held her hissed out sarcastically.

Jynx threw herself backwards without warning. The knife blade cut her skin, but she was suddenly free. She was on her hands and knees, trying to catch her breath.

Stone jumped the man and rolled him the opposite direction from Jynx. He punched the man hard in the face. "Tell me who you're working for." He punched him again, making the man's face jerk to the side from the force of the hits.

"I'm not talking," the man yelled.

"Okay then. That's your call, buddy." And Stone grabbed him and put him in a chokehold until the attacker was unconscious. That was Stone being good. When all he really wanted to do was kill the man for putting his hands on Jynx. He punched him once more and then kicked him hard in the ribs. "Asshole." He spit next to him.

Stone walked over to Jynx and scooped her up in his arms. "You okay?"

Jynx stuck her head in his neck and wrapped her arms around him. "Yes. I'm fine."

"Let's get out of here before the cops show up." Stone started towards her truck. "This is yours I take it?"

"Yes, she's mine, but we can't go back yet, I have someplace I want to drop them off. I'll meet you back at the house." Jynx opened up a side compartment of the truck and pulled out some rope. "I, Watson, have an idea."

"Well I'm not going home, so you might as well clue me in on your idea." Stone folded his arms, displaying his determination.

"I was hoping you would say that. You might change your mind once you find out where we're headed. They should be unconscious for at least an hour, so we have fifteen minutes in and out without being seen or killed. Got it?" Jynx talked while she handed Stone the ropes. "Before you tie them up, I want to leave them in just their boxers."

"Great idea." Stone laughed and started to undress the other guy. "What happens if they're not wearing any boxers?"

"I guess they'll be going commando," Jynx replied shrugging her shoulders and laughed.

Once the three men were piled in the back of her truck with Fusion watching over them, Jynx jumped in the drivers seat and waited for Stone to pull up next to Newton. They drove through the light traffic with ease, when she decided to pull over and stopped. In her rearview mirror she watched Stone pulling up to the window. They were parked down the street from the Creole Kane Sugar warehouse.

"What are we doing here?" Stone questioned.

"We're making a delivery." Jynx nodded her head towards a small building along-side the river. The building itself actually protruded over the water before you actually reached the warehouse. It was the easiest way to leave the men behind without getting caught.

There was no room for error or she'd end up dead like her father. With the money she collected she prepared and organized everything in great detail to give herself every option of success. She trusted Stone. He was the good guy and becoming Gambino's target he was forced into her secret life. Now, she put him in even more danger by having him with her. She reached underneath the cushion of her seat to a hidden compartment. A door opened and pushed out a bracket holding her I-pad. The brace was fancy with brass fittings, cogs, dials, and gears all put together precisely, making it look elegant and vintage.

Quickly she typed something and waited.

"What are you doing?"

"I just sent a command that's going jam all their camera's and auto lock the doors so no one can exit the building and at the same time disable the phone lines and cell phones. Newton, check and make sure everything is locked down so we can pull up to the door."

"All is clear," Newton responded.

"Okay we have five minutes to drop them off at the door and get out." Jynx looked at Stone. "Ready?"

"Yes indeed!" Stone laughed.

"Let's go." She laughed as she jumped out the truck. "I wish I could be here when they find their men."

Without delay, Jynx went to the first man closest to her and started to pull him out. She noticed Stone move right next to her and bodily pulled the men from the back of the truck and deposited them sitting in a circle at the door. He made sure their gags were tight and ropes snug.

"Let's go!" Jynx leading the way jumped into her truck and pulled off, nice and quiet like. She watched Stone on Newton pull up to her window.

"Jynx, we need to talk."

Chapter 5

"Oh yeah! I'm in big trouble now," Jynx mumbled to herself. *At least when I mess up, I do it royally*, she thought in disgust.

One, she'd had sex, which wasn't the real problem. The problem was she had just lost her virginity. Who at age twenty-eight was still a virgin? She tried not to look out the van window and see how good he fit on Newton. They made the perfect team. They all fit together like the perfect puzzle.

"Damn it!" she hissed. *I have to stop doing this to myself. One, he can't be mine. Two, when he does find out who I am, and that it was me, Jynx slash Merrick, the attorney who got Gambino off and got him shot. Holy crapolla I am doomed. Three, once he finds out that I have been living a double life, attorney slash some kind of vigilante, what will he do? Will he blow me out the water? Go to the police? I could lose my license as a lawyer.*

"Oh what a tangled web I weave." Her sarcastic humor on the rise, she giggled from all the stress.

The heaviness suddenly hit her chest like a ton of bricks. "I should have never brought him home." At a red light she put her head against the steering wheel.

"Fuck me!" Suddenly she thought of another problem. "Why did Gambino send his goons to attack me, the Jynx persona? He doesn't know we're one and the same." But that was easy to answer. He was trying to get to Merrick through Jynx, thinking she was her weak link. It's a busy street and Gambino could easily have had someone watching the house. "Stupid asshole. How dare Gambino fuck with me like that!" she fumed. "How dare him!"

Stone wasn't stupid. She needed to take his mind off what he thought he knew and send him in another direction. "Hey, Stone, follow me," she told him through the open window. For more than one reason she decided it wasn't safe to go back to the house.

With the new plan in action she pulled into a grocery store parking lot to grab a few things. She only went to the birdhouse when she was in need. "Fusion girl, watch the parking lot in case we were followed, okay? I think we're safe but we still should be cautious to make sure we weren't."

Fusion opened her mouth and a small bird drone flew out into the air.

Jynx jumped out to meet Newton and Stone. "Newton, I need you to lock the house down, transfer the camera recordings to the birdhouse, and prepare for departure. It's not safe to go back to the house right now. We need to lay low for a while. If anyone penetrates the house, burn it down with him or her inside.

"We need to pick up some food and supplies. If they're on their game, we'll be sitting ducks. They will want to know about Jynx. And you know I just pissed in their wheatie's."

"So," he paused, "you know who's behind the attack?"

"Yes. I think I do, but that's neither here nor there. We just need to lose ourselves under the radar. Are you with me?"

"Yes, and yes, they weren't expecting you to fight back," Stone said. "Okay, let's go shopping.

The store smelled like a florist when Jynx walked in the entrance. Fresh cut flowers were sitting in different cubicles so people could make their own arrangements.

She noticed he stopped at the flowers. "What are you doing?"

"I was going to get you some flowers."

Jynx turned slowly and gave him a weird look. "Do I look like the flowers kind of girl? Really?" She laughed impishly, rolling her eyes.

"I guess not. I was trying to show my appreciation."

"Thank you for the gesture, but it's ok." Now she wondered if he was trying to show his appreciation over the virgin thing or keeping him safe? She didn't want to think too hard on the virgin part. No, she wouldn't think like that.

Making a quick trip through the grocery store, Jynx bought enough supplies for a few days and paid with cash. Jynx exited the store and started walking in the opposite direction.

"Where are you going? The truck is this way." Stone pointed to front of the store.

"No, it's not." She laughed when she saw the confusion cross his features. "Follow me."

At the back of the store where deliveries were made, a few truck cargo containers were parked alongside each other for storage. A eighteen wheeler was parked among a mass of storage containers. Stone caught a glimpse of the Volkswagen being loaded inside the rig. A few women were standing outside of it wearing maid outfits.

A woman wearing a black business suit and glasses with her hair pulled back started to approach her when Jynx waved. Jynx stopped in front of the stranger and shook her hand. "Hi, Susan."

The woman looked at Stone over the rim of her glasses at Stone giving him the up and down look with a questioning look towards Jynx.

"Will you excuse us for a second beefcake?" Without waiting for an answer, the woman identified as Susan guided Jynx away without waiting for a response.

"You know I don't get into your business,, ole' girl nor do I ever question your methods, but you have never, ever had someone with you or had to use the code word."

"I know, Pauline. I used the code word so you wouldn't just start talking. He doesn't know."

"I know my job is just to clean up, but we have this understanding between the two of us. You helped me long ago, and we both have been cleaning up the streets of New Orleans for years now. So I tell you this out of respect. Call me if you get in a pinch."

"Thank you. I think I'm okay for now. Gambino is trouble so be careful. He's trying to get to Merrick through me."

"He'd shit his fancy drawers if he knew Merrick was you." Pauline laughed.

"Make sure it's safe before you send the girls to clean the house. I don't want anyone hurt because of me."

"Yes, I'm already on it. I have someone watching them, watching the house. I just want you to be careful."

"Oh, and by the way, this one is sure easy on the eyes."

Jynx smiled. "I'll be in touch." Jynx turned towards Stone, dismissing her.

She tried to read Stone's expression, wondering what he was thinking, but he was good at keeping his thoughts to himself. All it did was put knots in her belly as she approached. Funny though it matters what he thinks of her when no one else's does.

"Is everything in order?" Jynx asked.

Newton just looked like an ordinary parked motorcycle, but she knew he waiting for her to approach.

"Fusion is in the white Tahoe. Everything is prepared, the birdhouse lights and water are now on, awaiting your arrival."

"You ride Newton. He'll get you where you need to be, and I'll be right behind you. I'm exhausted."

She was a little surprised when Stone grabbed her around the waist and pulled her roughly against him, making her look up at him. That was her mistake. Her conscious fought the urge to wrap her arms around his neck. Instead she pulled away slightly, and inside she wasn't disappointed when he didn't release her.

"Who are you really?" he demanded. "And before you lie to me, just know I'm not stupid. No one I know has cars and toys like yours, or maids." he demanded.

"All I'm going to say is that you already know too much, and I'm not comfortable with that. Truth be told, I should have taken you to the hospital. Instead you left the house, endangering yourself even more. Those men will report to Gambino. I need to regroup, and it's not safe for us to be on the street or return to the house unprepared." She watched his features harden with disappointment.

"Don't look like that. I'd do it all over again if that meant you would be safe."

"Why does it matter so much to you if I'm safe, or dead for that matter?" He asked.

"It just does. Isn't that enough?" Jynx started to squirm in his arms, but he tightened his grip. She looked up in question.

His lips were warm and possessive when they touched hers, and she felt the tingles ignite. Her belly knotted, her nipples hardened with the sudden fire burning in her veins. His hand went to the back of her head, holding her in place, and that possessiveness made her legs turn to butter. His tongue slipped in demanding a response and she couldn't fight the need burning through her. Deep down she didn't want to. Her toes curled. Jynx leaned into him needing more, wanting more. At some point she remembered where she was and pulled away.

Her hand went to her dreads in a self-conscious motion. "We really need to get off the street." Jynx pulled against his embrace, and he finally released his hold. The loss of his touch filled her suddenly, catching her off-guard. She tripped over her own feet.

"You okay, Jynx?" Stone asked suddenly.

"What?" she asked confused.

"You tripped, and you look like I hurt you. Are you okay?" he asked again.

Flustered, she replied, "Yeah, I'm fine." Dismissing the concern offhandedly and feeling awkward, she stumbled toward the GMC.

He was making her feel emotions that had been buried with her father. As a small child she had been a daddy's girl. The last summer she'd ever played baseball, she had been chosen to play all-stars. Her dad had been so proud and excited that he took her out to get ice cream. Someone had brutally killed her father in front of her eyes while she had been eating her ice cream.

To this day she couldn't stand the sight of ice cream. "Ready?" She called out to Stone, who was already sitting on Newton.

"Waiting on you, babe," Stone announced.

Newton purred loudly in answer and Fusion growled low in her throat from the backseat.

"Well then, let's roll. I have to make a quick stop. It'll only take a moment, so just wait for me." Jynx started out with Fusion, and Stone followed behind on Newton. It didn't take long to get to Bourbon Street where it would be easy to get lost among the swarms of people. She considered this her advantage.

She stopped at an electronic store to buy a prepaid phone and had it activated with a bogus identity.

She pulled up at an old two-story building that had recently seen a new coat of paint. Upstairs the shutters offset the ugliness of the building. The building was old, maybe historical, but nothing to brag about. The paint didn't do it any justice.

Jynx stepped out and watched as Stone dismounted from Newton. The man's body flexed and moved from an inner strength. Sculpted perfectly with muscles, he was beautiful and held himself with honor. The way he carried himself made her weak in the knees. She watched him approach with a smile on his lips.

"Where might we be?"

His curious expression made her grin. "You can follow me." She opened the back door, do you want me to cover you, or go invisible? Fusion nosed the cover. Ok girl. Merrick leaned in to cover Fusion with a sheet. "Just for a few moments, Fusion, so I can get you inside."

"She wants Stone to carry her,mistress." Newton stated.

"Leave her to me. I'll carry her."

"How can I deny her?"

He nodded his head, and she backed off to open the door using a key to unlock the ironwork guard door. Once they were inside she shut the door trying not to think how Fusion wanted Stone to carry her. *A part of her thought, could she be flirting, but how could that be when she's a machine.*

The door locks automatically. Merrick caught his amazed expression. "What?" She wanted to know what he was thinking.

"You wouldn't expect this from looking at the outside of this place," he said in awe.

The breezeway ceiling was at least fifteen feet tall. Under their feet were huge stones cemented into place. Straight through the breezeway led to an enormous courtyard with wrought iron benches and plants. Most of the ground was brick and stone which gave the place the old New Orleans look. Along the left side were a few sets of French doors and straight ahead lead to other condos.

Jynx went through another archway and up some stairs. At the landing there were two doors. The first door to the left side was considered one apartment,and another way led to other apartments. Jynx unlocked the first door and turned and held it open for Stone and Fusion to pass through.

"I'll be back. I need to get Newton off the street. He's one of a kind, and leaving him in the open would be like putting a bull's-eye on us. Don't open the door. I'll let myself in." She locked the door and went down the stairs.

When she stepped out into the street, she felt eyes on her, and as she looked up to her balcony, Stone was there looking up and down the street, watching her back. Jynx smiled. "I'll be right up."

She grabbed Newton by the handlebars, but really the bike rolled on its own accord. Once through the doors into the breezeway, she removed her hands and allowed Newton to move freely. "Put your invisible shield up and keep a lookout. If you need me just let me know. Do you need anything, big guy?"

"No. I'll keep the perimeter under surveillance and determine if there are any problems," Newton stated. His body flickered and disappeared.

"Watching you do that never gets old." She shook her head and patted his seat before turning away and heading back upstairs. Jynx leaned against the door, exhausted. The weight of today's trouble and all the ramifications slammed into her thoughts, suddenly overwhelming her. Tears smarted behind her closed eyes, but she defied herself the pleasure of release. Now was not the time to feel weakness, she needed to be strong, wise. Above all else, Jynx needed to stay one step ahead of Gambino, or else both she and Stone would end up dead.

"You okay?"

She opened her eyes to find Stone standing over her, looking concerned.

"Yes. It's just been a day."

To prove it, she pushed herself from the support of the door, walked straight to the kitchen counter, and started to unload the groceries.

"Are you ready to eat now or relax? Gosh, did that sound all domestic or what?" Jynx asked, trying to challenge him into a different conversation than what might be on his mind. She watched him as he picked up a handful of grapes.

"You know we really need to talk, but I'll let it wait. I can tell you're dead on your feet. Let's relax and later I'll help you whip us up something to eat."

"I am really drained. I'm sorry." Jynx avoided looking into his eyes.

"Sorry? For what? Keeping me safe? Don't do that. I owe you everything. It's not like you're the attorney who got Gambino off!"

Jynx cringed from the mental slap in the face. Before he saw how his words hit a nerve, she turned away. Her knees wobbled, and she felt like he had just sucker punched her with his words.

"Whose place is this?"

"Mine. You'll be safe here. We can figure out a game plan later. Okay?" Her voice came out small, the hurt showing through. Jynx didn't allow him to answer. "I need a nap." Really she needed to regroup. She needed a moment to lick her wounds. For the first time she had allowed herself to fall for someone. After all was said and done, she knew she would pay the price. At the moment she just wanted, needed to be alone. "Fusion will guard us, and Newton is downstairs, incognito."

"I wish I had brought my briefcase. I can't believe I left it behind yet again. That is so unlike me. It makes me feel unprotected," Stone complained.

"Well, let me fix that right up for you. Follow me, sir". Jynx opened up her big pantry door, and Stone leaned over her, peering over her shoulder. She lifted a brass plate that revealed a screen. When she put her hand on it, an L.E.D. keyboard appeared. She entered a code, and the pantry wall swung open, flush against one of the other walls to reveal a small secret room. Each wall held all sorts of guns, knives, and some unrecognizable weapons. Ammo sat in boxes under a small table and against the walls, at least waist high.

The table held objects that looked like a bird, a beetle, and a frog. A variety of drones hung from the ceiling. In the small room there wasn't any wasted space.

The noise behind her alerted Jynx. Without turning to look at his face, she knew she had impressed him once again. "Would you like to come play with my toys?" Jynx asked politely.

"You know I do. I don't know who you are, lady, but I'm just glad you're on my side."

"I could almost say you don't need any weapons. You're a lethal deterrent all by yourself. I saw how you took those guys out without blinking an eye. You're deadly. Armed with weapons you'll be unstoppable.

"I'm going to bed. If you want to play Lone Ranger, just don't leave the apartment. I don't need any snitches calling us in to Gambino, understand? I'm going to run out of hiding places. I'll give you a tour later, or you can go look around by yourself."

She dragged herself up the stairs. Jynx could almost feel the pillow under her face. *Forget the shower, I'll take one later.* Right now all she wanted was to shut her eyes. Worry and concern made her muscles bunch in knots. The ass. Sometimes masterminds couldn't think past their own stupidity.

Before she did anything, she opened up the French doors leading to her personal balcony. It was narrow but it ran the length of her room to the next bedroom.

All afternoon dark clouds had been gathering overhead. Lightning streaked across the horizon in a brilliant display of electronic spark, heating up the sky. The thunder rocked the ground with its intensity. No rain yet, but she could smell it in the air, a warning of what was to come.

Jynx stripped off her clothes and pulled a t-shirt nightgown over her head and shoulders. From the bag she had brought into the room, she pulled out the package, opened the box, and pulled out the untraceable prepaid cell phone.

A bit nervous she tapped the voice video chat icon and waited until it opened so she could sign in and input her mother's information. Anxious, she sat on the rug at the terrace door and allowed her legs to stretch out. Her wiggled her toes, letting them rest on the balcony.

"Hello," her mother's image appeared and her voice sounded so full of love.

"Momma?" Jynx clenched the phone tighter when she saw her mother's anxious face.

"Merrick, honey? I've been so worried," the voice choked.

Merrick smiled through the tears.

"Oh, Momma," Jynx started to cry in earnest. "Are you safe?" Jynx asked in between hiccups.

"Sunflowers." It was their code to alert the other that it was safe and that it was clear to talk. Jynx had come up with the code when she put her mother in hiding. It was her mother's favorite flower. "The news said..." The worried voice wobbled.

"Mom, please don't cry. I'm all right."

At least for now, she thought. She couldn't tell her mom that. It would only make her worry, so instead she lied.

"I wanted to call to let you know that I'm safe and how much I love you, Momma."

"Your father would be so proud." Her mother's smile shown through her tears.

Jynx loved that smile. It reminded her of the few times they could be happy.

"Be careful, mom. I've made some pretty powerful enemies lately. More than my normal." A strained giggle escaped. "You know me. I love to stir the pot, so don't talk to strangers."

"Are you in over your head, darling?"

Merrick couldn't bear to hear the worry in her mom's voice. "No, Momma. I'll find my way. I always do." She didn't want her mother to worry anymore than she already did. As a result the little white lies fell from her lips easily. Jynx would do anything to protect her mother. On a website there are quotes cards people shared online, and one stuck in her mind. "For family, I'd bury a body."

"I love you more than the darkness in the night sky. Do you need anything, Mom? Tell me quickly."

"No, my darling. You send too much now."

"I have to go now." Jynx watched her mother's hand come up as if to stop her from hanging up. The tears rolled down her aged face, but she smiled through it all.

Her own eyes burned with sorrow and great waves of loneliness enveloped her as she hung up. In a rare occurrence, Jynx collapsed back into her room onto the floor and finally gave in to the tears. Thunder roared, announcing the rain. A heavy drop fell and another until, within seconds, it was pouring, almost as much as her heart was pouring out her anguish.

The heavy rain penetrated through the open antique French door to drench her and the antique floors surrounding her. Her heart ached for all the lonely years. The life without her father's presence, all that was left were his memories and one big nightmare. She'd give anything if her father could still be there.

The traumatic dream of the day she lost her dad was always a constant reminder of why she pushed herself. To see Anthony Gambino in jail, or dead. He wasn't going to get to her mother, or the people she loved. He was a animal, destroying anyone in his path. The isolation from her mother and the loneliness was all for her father and what he had been trying to accomplish, in addition to keeping her mother safe and out of Gambino's hands.

Today, yesterday, ever since the verdict had been announced, Jynx felt like she had failed somehow. Especially arriving at Stone's residence to find him shot and fighting for his life. The guilt was suffocating, but she'd die to keep him safe. It was her responsibility because it was all her fault that the mafia crime lord was after him. She should have let Gambino go to jail, but in all honesty as powerful as he was, he would have run things from behind bars. All it would have been was an inconvenience.

The sudden stillness from the lack of rain pelting against her body made her raise her head to peer outside only to find Stone standing drenched in the doorway, shielding her from the onslaught of rain. It made a involuntary chill take claim over her body. Bare-chested he stood wearing only rain soaked jeans hugging his muscular hips. His muscles flexed with his movements. Stone's skin glistened from the water running down his chest.

Her belly tightened with awareness. He was truly beautiful, perfect standing over her like some guardian, looking powerful and intimidating. Water dripped from his chin, but it was the burning look that made a quiet gasp escape from her lips, leaving her wordless. Her nipples hardened under her nightgown. Her skin felt overly sensitive with the need to have him touch her, but she'd bite off her tongue before she would tell him.

"No!" Jynx screamed. "You can't see me like this. Leave me. I beg you." She kicked out at him to force his compliance.

Chapter 6

Stone wanted to stop her from going to her room. He wanted to get to know her, but he knew after everything that had happened she was exhausted and needed some rest. He had never met anyone like her before. She was so guarded the way she protected herself and her toys. His gut said CIA, or something along those lines. Military background was a good possibility. All he knew was she was prepared for just about anything.

He walked over to the big French doors and stood just inside, watching the rainfall. It was turning out to be a bad storm. The sky was dark and heavy with grey clouds. That was when he heard her talking quietly and it caught his attention. The hairs on his arms stood up when he heard her crying. Everything in him went on alert. Whoever she was talking to upset her enough to make her fall apart.

Instantly he was pissed and not just a little. His need to protect her like she had been breaking her little neck to protect him made him walk out on the second floor balcony to listen. The rain pummeled him with water, instantly soaking his body, but he didn't care. All he knew was that his little Jynx was upstairs upset and he couldn't hear above the rain except for the soft murmur of her voice.

With determination he ran back inside hitting the stairs two at a time. He jumped the last two to get to the upper floor. He tried the first door and it was locked. Another door stood open, and he ran quickly through which lead him to the closed French doors. Stone opened them with such force the glass rattled in distress.

He stepped onto the balcony and ran across to the only other opening and stopped dead in his tracks at what he witnessed.

Jynx lay sprawled out on the floor with a long T-shirt nightgown plastered to her body. She covered her face with her hands as she cried brokenly. Her dreads spread out against the floor like a black fan. In that

moment, Stone realized he was in love with
her.

"Go away!" Jynx screamed.

He smiled as she kicked out at him in
defiance.

"That's not going to happen little
lady." Stone reached down and gently picked
her up and cradled her body against his chest.
At first she struggled against him, beating at
his chest.

"Put me down."

"For once let someone other than
yourself care for you. I know it's a novelty,
but allow me the simple pleasure." She weighed
hardly anything for such a dynamo package that
she was as a woman. Jynx had a stronger will
than some of the military men he had worked
with. He would fight next to Jynx anytime
knowing she'd have his back.

Finally she looked up into his eyes, and
he became lost in her green gaze. In that
moment Stone realized how fragile she was, and
his protectiveness raised to the occasion, and
something more. He smiled as he watched Jynx
put her arms around his neck and laid her head
against his shoulder.

He leaned down and touched his lips to
hers because he couldn't stop himself. The
kiss was supposed to offer comfort, but when
her mouth opened to his and her tongue
entered, Stone became dominant, demanding,
coaching her with his mouth. His body burned
as his hard cock strained against his jeans.

He glanced into her room to find a huge
canopy bed with thick elaborate detailed
bedposts. Material hung from the top at each
corner and twisted into a rope to wrap around
each post. Billows of material hung over the
top enclosing it to protect when the mosquito
netting was released.

On the floor he noticed a box with a
picture of a prepaid phone. With a purpose, he
kicked it out of his way to lay her gently
upon her bed. He looked down at her lying
there and Stone couldn't get enough of looking

at her. She was beautiful and had all the right curves. He covered her with his body quickly so she wouldn't change her mind and bent down to fuse his lips to hers while he sucked on her tongue. He grabbed the nightgown and released her tongue long enough to pull it over her head. Her perk nipples stood at attention, begging his touch. His mouth went to one and he nibbled and suckled. His other hand grabbed her other breast rolling the nipple between his fingers.

Her moan egged him on, and he gently pinched the nipple in his hand. Her torso bucked off the bed. Her hands grabbed his head to pull him closer, a signal she wanted more. He pulled her hands above her head holding her still, and kissed her deeply, biting her bottom lip. Her body squirmed under him. His hands touched everywhere, traveling along her body, and his lips followed kissing and nipping.

His hand moved lower to between her legs and moving lower checking to see if she was ready for him. His fingers pushed under her underwear to find her sex hot and wet. Her body came off the bed to meet his hand. The sound of her whimper rippled through him like music, as he trailed kisses over a tattoo along her ribcage. He was past his patience, all he wanted was to taste her.

Stone pulled her panties down her legs slowly, nibbling and kissing her inner thighs. After he removed her panties, he took her foot and put her toe in his mouth and sucked. Listening to her unguarded whimpers, moans and gasps was music to his ears.

Rising to his knees, he pulled up and away taking, a foot in each hand, spreading her legs wide open and toward her head, holding her in a submissive position. Her pussy was opened to him to do as he pleased, clean shaven and pink. Her little nubbin peeked out and Stone's mouth watered.

He had to taste her. Stone quickly moved his face above her wet sex and ran his tongue

over her swollen clit. Unrelenting in his
assault, Stone held her legs wide apart as he
allowed his breath to blow on her aroused sex.
Her body bowed upwards, toward his face. He
closed his mouth over her sex and suckled and
licked. Stone watched as her head thrashed
from side to side and her hands fisted in the
bedspread.

"Please," her voice was hoarse.

He heard her beg, and that made his cock
even harder. He raised his head, searching her
face.

"Please what? What is it you want?"
Stone teased.

Without waiting for her reply, Stone
showed no mercy as he slowly licked down her
sex towards her ass. Involuntary her body
bucked against his hand. Stone held firm and
continued his attention to the forbidden
treasure. When her body became accustomed and
she relaxed somewhat. That was his cue Stone
slipped his tongue inside.

She gasped.

Her body went rigid in his hands as she
came apart. Quickly before she finished, he
moved to her sex and licked and sucked. Her
hands fisted in his hair, burying his face
closer. When she collapsed, he released her
legs and fought to get his wet jeans down his
legs.

His hard cock sprang to attention as he
moved between her thighs. Stone entered her
quickly, impaling his shaft deep inside her in
one quick thrust. His head rolled backwards
and his eyes closed as her tight walls closed
around his shaft. The feeling of ecstasy
ripped through him like a tidal wave. After a
few moments of bliss Stone pulled himself
almost out and then entered her swiftly once
again, burying deep. Jynx was so tight he
savored the sensations and kept his strokes
steady with a purpose to show her pleasure and
to shower her with love.

Goodness, where did that come from? He
shouldn't allow himself to have those

feelings. Her hips met his every thrust, keeping pace with him. She was so tight, so hot pulling at his cock. She was screaming out in pleasure moving harder, faster. Stone met her urgent thrust, and she tensed up and came apart once again screaming out. He came with her, spilling his seed as he collapsed against her. Stone reached down and kissed her lips, nibbling at her bottom lip until he coached a reaction.

Stone reached for the blanket to cover them, pulling her close against his body, snuggling with her. He kissed her forehead and heard her sigh. He noticed her eyes were closed and her breathing had slowed. He closed his eyes, allowing sleep to pull him under.

When Stone opened his eyes, the room was in darkness and Jynx was still sleeping. His stomach grumbled, reminding him they hadn't eaten. Actually now that he thought about it, he hadn't seen Jynx eat anything since he had met her. Her hand was lying across his chest, so he removed it with great care so as not to wake her. Then he silently slipped out of bed silently.

He found his jeans on the floor, and they were dripping wet. No way he was going to wear them that way, so he carried them from the room. In the kitchen Stone found the laundry room and removed the contents of his pockets and threw his pants in the dryer. He grabbed a towel and closed the door, keeping the noise at a minimum.

It was really late to cook anything on the heavy side, so maybe he would whip up some breakfast stuff. Stone rummaged through the cabinets and refrigerator to see what he could work with to make them something edible.

Stone smiled and realized how happy he was at the moment. Jynx had gotten under his skin quickly and without any warning. Watching his buddies die and leaving families behind kept him from being in a serious relationship.

He never received mail, or had to make a phone call. He didn't want that kind of life for himself. The military had been his family at least until he retired. Now, what was he going to do? When he was shot at the coffee shop, he'd only been home for eight hours and he had been on his way to see his parents before all hell broke loose. When Stone had opened his eyes his mother was hanging over his bed with tears in her eyes. His dad was leaning over the other side. Tubes ran from his body and he felt like the Hulk threw him around like a rag doll.

Not only that they had heavy security at the door which puzzled him. At first he didn't remember what had happened. It took a minute for his brain to function and to put the pieces together. He'd been shot on U.S. soil.

It turned out the person who shot him and a woman at the cafe was mafia, and Stone was an eyewitness. The woman turned out to be a senator's wife, and the shooter didn't count on him being there interrupting his plans. Stone had tried to protect her using his own body as a shield.

Then he'd been shot after the trial. Stone had slipped away from security and headed home to grab some stuff. His goal had been to head to base to beg his caption to send him back out, but they had been waiting on him.

If it hand't been for Jynx and her sidekicks, Stone knew he would be dead. The little spitfire was hell on wheels and he loved that about her. She showed no weakness and fought for everything. He had to admit he admired her guts. Stone smiled. She was soft too, with a sense of humor and smart. He'd never met anyone like her before.

He realized she was hiding stuff from him. Stone knew deep down it was a protection measure on her part. It was how she stayed alive. This girl didn't trust anyone. Damn, she was a woman and she was playing a deadly game of cat and mouse trying to keep him safe.

When she allowed her guard down and let Stone in her world, the attraction, and feelings hit him in his secret places that he locked up. She got under his skin and he found himself wanting to protect her and her secrets and more. He wanted to be with her. Just the thought of him walking away, going back into the field wasn't an option.

Stone shook his head and grabbed some bread, eggs and cinnamon. In a skillet he fried up some ham slices and made quick work of French toast. While it was cooking he poured some syrup in a coffee cup and put into the microwave and heated it up. After grabbing two glasses, he poured orange juice and fixed her plate.

When he turned to bring her the plate of food, Jynx was standing right behind him. She came into the room without a sound. She was smiling up at him, shyly.

"Why didn't you wake me? I could have done this for us."

"I wanted you to get some rest. You've been running around protecting me and stressing. I wanted to do something nice for you for a change.

"You didn't mind me in your kitchen did you? I'll clean up the mess."

"No, I don't mind at all, and no, you cooked, I clean."

He watched as she walked away with the plate in her hands and sat on the ground, Indian style, at the French doors and looked out into the rain. He followed her motions and sat right next to her with his knee touching hers. He wanted, no, he needed the contact. Stone wasn't by far an insecure person, but he never experienced this kind of need that drove him to keep trying. On so many occasions she shut him out because it was how she lived. Earning her trust wasn't going to be easy which only made him proud of her for being so cautious.

"I like the rain and the sound it makes when it's pouring. I don't care to drive in it though."

That small omission of something personal went a long way with him. "I like how it smells. Leaves everything fresh, like a new beginning." Stone watched her nod her head as she moved her food around on her plate with her fork. "You don't like French toast? I can make you something else if you like."

"Yes, I like it. I'm sorry. I was thinking." He watched as she took a bite and nodded in his direction.

"It's good."

"Thank you. I want to see it all gone because I don't remember when I seen you eat anything."

"Sometimes I get so caught up in stuff I forget to eat."

Stone couldn't help himself he leaned over and touched his lips to hers, needing to kiss her. He felt her take a breath of surprise but that didn't stop him as he pulled her bottom lip into his mouth and suckled it.

When the kiss ended, he released her lip and glanced down at her face. For a brief moment her eyes were closed. Jynx's eyelids fluttered open and he lost himself in the green of her eyes. His gut danced and his blood rushed through his body. The sensations smashing through him right now were all new to him. If Stone were honest with himself, he had to admit he couldn't get his fill.

"You had some syrup on your lips," he said, "and we don't have napkins." Stone wiggled his eyebrows playfully.

"You do, too."

Before Stone understood her words, she raised up on her knees and her lips were on his. She drew his bottom lip into her mouth and nibbled. His body came to full attention under the towel.

Stone watched her eyes connect to his and unexpectedly her hand brushed against his arousal hidden beneath the towel. Stone's breath caught in his throat, leaving him speechless as her fingers closed around his cock, squeezing him firmly.

A moan escaped before he could stop it. Before he dumped his breakfast, he put down his plate and the coffee cup of syrup he had brought with him. Her hand moved under the towel while he was leaning over to empty his hands. Now she grasped him in a firm grip and pumped him up and down, making him rock hard.

"Oh, you like that, do you?"

"Yes," he replied through gritted teeth.

She opened the towel more for better access with her other hand and leaned down and put him in her mouth. Stone moved his legs out from under him, giving her easier access. Her tongue was soft as it swirled around his shaft inside her mouth, making his hips come off the floor.

Her dreads hid what she was doing, and she raised off him for a second before he felt very warm syrup being poured over him.

"Oh." It came out as a long and drawn surprise.

Her lips enclosed his cock with sucking pressure. As her tongue swirled and licked, her fingers wrapped around his balls, gently massaging them as she devoured the syrup. Her tongue worked magic, licking up and down his shaft.

He pulled her gently from on top of him, taking her lips into his.

"My turn." He pushed her to the floor, straddling her hips. Stone grabbed her hands and moved them above her head, holding them prisoner.

"Pretend your hands are tied and don't move them for any reason. Understand?"

Stone waited until she agreed before he moved his body along side of hers, leaving her open for his pleasure. He kissed her lips hungrily, tasting the syrup on her lips, then moved to her neck where he sucked and bit, leaving his mark.

His hand kept hers above her head and held her in place while he could still hold her in place. Her body bowed up to him, begging for attention, and her nipples showed her arousal with hardened buds. Stone blew his heated breath against one, causing her to shiver as he took the nub into his mouth and nipped the bud, drawing a loud moan.

Under him she lifted her body for his touch, but he only moved his hand to the other breast and rolled the nipple between two fingers.

"Please," she begged.

"Tell me. I want you to tell me what you want." His fingers traveled over her body with slow movements, raising goose bumps on her body. His hand stopped over her cleaned shaven pussy and added a little pressure against her and rubbed.

"I want you!" she cried out.

His fingers opened the folds covering her sweet pussy and found she was wet and ready. Still he waited even though he wanted to drive into her hard and fast. Stone wanted to drive her insane with need.

"Now, Stone, I want you inside me now!" Jynx screamed out.

"Put your feet over my shoulders." When he felt her hesitate, Stone ordered hoarsely. "Do it now."

When she lifted her legs to oblige, he helped her until her legs were where he wanted them. This position brought her body closer and he rubbed her swollen sex with a finger before he moved the head of his shaft over her opening, adding a slight pressure. Jynx tried to grind herself against his manhood. Still he pulled back. When she moved her hands from behind her head. "I didn't tell you Jynx you could move your hands," Stone warned. "Put them back." The sound of the slap against the cheek of her ass thrilled him. Her scream was an endearment. Then he massaged the area he spanked soothing the sting.

He was the one in control and as punishment he denied her what she wanted most. Stone wanted her to surrender herself into his care. She controlled many things on the streets, but in bed he was her master. The whimpers, the moans and watching how her head thrashed from side to side, he waited.

"Please." she begged. Her body thrashed against his touch, a light red rash appeared above her breast.

If Jynx wanted to tease, he'd show her, he was the master. Stone loved this position because he could watch her expressions change and her reactions to what he was doing as he moved over her clit.

"Please."

"What's my name?"

"Stone." She hissed as another spike of arousal flared.

"No. Not at this moment I'm not."

"Again, what's my name?" He rubbed the tip of his shaft against her opening.

"Stone." Jynx shouted.

She screamed out loud, when he slapped her other cheek. The sound bounced off the walls.

"Here, now, you call me, Master!"

"Master!" She shouted. "Master!"

Her submission did him in and he couldn't hold back any longer himself, he grasped her hips with his hands and entered her fully with one quick hard thrust.

"Yes!" Jynx screamed out loud. "More, harder I beg you," she wailed. Stone complied driving into her, hard, fast. The tight walls of her body squeezed him tight, urging him on with the mindless wonder of her body.

"Come now." Stone ordered, driving in and out repeatedly, watching the pleasure cross her face as her head moved from side to side. Stone watched her breasts jiggle and her body as well as her hands were still above her head. "Come for me now," he commanded once more, and this time he reached down to one of her breast, and as her body tightened in the beginning of her orgasm, he pinched her nipple as his body pounded her body as she reached her climax.

Her scream of pleasure and her body clenching against his own swollen manhood sent him over the edge in his own climax. Stone kept pace until only ripples rocked their bodies. He leaned over and kissed her lips. "You may move your arms now." Stone's out of breath comment came out in a rush of air.

Stone gathered Jynx against him as their heart rates slowed, listening to the downpour outside. Rain came into the opened french doors, pelting them with cold water. It was a pleasant sensation against the heat of summer.

Time seemed to slow down, or maybe he dozed, but Jynx was fast asleep with her head pillowed on his shoulder. Trying not to wake her, Stone maneuvered his body with great care from underneath Jynx's. Once he was free Stone stood over her for a moment, admiring her without that cheeky look she'd give him. He didn't want to admit it to himself, but deep down Stone realized that he probably was falling for her.

With great care as not to awaken her, Stone slid one arm under her knees and the other under her back and lifted her easily up to cradle her against his chest. Her eyes opened temperately and she smiled as she laid her head against his shoulder and once again she was asleep.

Stone stood there for a moment to make sure she was sleeping deeply before he moved. When he was satisfied, he walked up the stairs, taking one step at a time until he reached the top foyer where there was a hall tree with a small lamp. He entered her bedroom and laid her on her bed and pulled the top sheet over her body to cover her. The French door to her room was still open and the breeze lightly chased the humidity of New Orleans away, making the room comfortable. He climbed in next to her under the sheet, pulling her against him to spoon and wrapping his arm around her waist.

Both of them awoke sitting upright in bed looking at each other in the dark. The

first thing Stone noticed there was no longer
and light coming in from the streetlight. The
small lamp was off from the hallway tree. It
was so dark he couldn't make out Jynx sitting
right next to him, but he felt her start to
move.

"Did you hear that? Was that inside or
out?" Jynx whispered softly in his ear.

He put his finger against her lips to
make her understand to be quiet. He grasped
her head and moved it up and down to show he
did know. It was too late, he should have
known she'd get up. The bump came unexpectedly
with her shoving a handgun into his hands.
Stone stood to investigate.

Stone could hear Fusion downstairs
attacking someone. Before he could react
someone punched him, knocking him into the
wall with a grunt. "Son of a bitch. Sneak me
will ya punk?" He grabbed the assailant behind
the head and punched him in his gut. When the
man bent over, Stone grabbed his attacker by
the head and jerked it quickly, snapping his
opponent's neck without hesitation. He heard
Jynx fighting on the other side of the bed. He
heard a gun go off, and her assailant screamed
and then there was silence.

"Fuck, fuck, fuck!" Jynx cussed. "Come
on. I'm starting to leave dead bodies
everywhere."

Fusion met them at the bedroom door. Her
assailant was curled up on the ground,
whimpering in pain from the bite marks from
the nails that were her teeth. The spring from
her jaw gave her a formidable lock down
pressure to the point of tearing flesh.

Before they went downstairs Stone went
to the cabinet and opened the door an
emergency light came on illuminating the
closet as Stone pulled out some more weapons.
"I'm not sure where we're going or who we'll
run into, but we need to be prepared. This is
some bullshit." Stone jerked items off the
shelf in frustration.

"I agree. This is bullshit, and I'm tired of running."

Stone watched her grab a duffle bag and started pulling weapons off the racks and things off the table. He still was amazed at the armory she held in her possession. "Let's go."

Downstairs Newton also had demobilized several men with sleeping darts leaving them sprawled out on the ground. The illusion of being invisible had given Newton an advantage over his assailants weaving in and out without being seen.

"Hop on Newton. We need to get out of here. Fusion jump. on Stone and he'll hold you." Newton pulled out into the drizzling rain. Jynx drove while Stone carried the duffle bag across his back and Fusion on his lap.

"We have to get out of town for a minute. We need to regroup and I need some sleep. Let's go to the shack, Newton. We need to rest up while I think of a plan of action."

"Come on I can hear the sirens coming in hard and loud. Someone must have called the cops," Stone said.

"It was I, "Newton confessed. "I alerted the police that the house had been broken into and the men downstairs were responsible for the dead upstairs."

"I couldn't have done better, Newton. Good job." Stone was impressed. They really worked as a team, and he was the outsider. He'd show her, he could fit in though and be part of their unit. He had lived his life in the military, and he was trained how to become part of a team, to trust each other.

Chapter 7

They drove for about an hour away from the city. Jynx was tired and pissed off. She loved her apartment. It might take years before she could return safely to the loft, but that was just how things were now, and she couldn't worry about things so trivial.

She was soaked to the bone. Her clothes clung to her body in a wet mass even her dreads were heavy with rain. When they left the condo, it was only drizzling, but as soon as she started out, it started pouring again. Jynx just needed some sleep. Her eyelids were so heavy she was having a hard time keeping them opened.

Finally she spotted the road. No one was out and about at this hour of the morning except for the early-bird fisherman. Of course during the week there were many commuters that traveled from Mississippi to New Orleans. Those poor people awakened at an ungodly hour just for work. The sun was starting its change, with new colors of oranges and reds.

Everyone was quiet on the ride there. Newton pulled to a stop at the bottom of a raised house. Jynx put her head down for a moment, collecting her thoughts. "Newton, can you scan the perimeter? Make sure there is no one here."

"You called this a Shack?"

"It's clear." Newton reported.

"Come into the garage so you can get some rest as well, Newton. You have done well tonight. Thank you. As always you saved us you and Fusion.

"Can you tell if we were followed?" Jynx asked hesitantly, more than a little afraid to hear if they were.

"All is clear. We are safe. I'll keep a visual of the perimeter. No one will come close to you." Newton and Fusion went into the garage.

"Come on. "Let's go in. I don't know about you, but I'm beat. My eyes are so heavy I can't keep them open anymore. Once I get some sleep I'll be able to focus on what to do."

Jynx watched him carry the duffle bag full of weapons toward the stairs.

"It looks like I need to carry you up those stairs," Stone said half joking.

Jynx smiled. "I think I can make it, but not much farther," One step at a time she forced herself up the stairs. "At least it stopped raining." At the top of the wrap-around deck, she pulled out a keychain full of keys and after fumbling with a few she unlocked the door and moved to the side to allow Stone over the threshold.

She shut the door, leaving them in a small foyer. Jynx turned on a small lamp and quickly disarmed the house's security system. From the light shining off the lamp, she led Stone into a large opened living room with vaulted ceilings, with four-by-four wooden beams.

She watched Stone put the bag down and walk toward a set of glass French doors as she turned on another lamp. "It's been awhile since I've been here. Do you mind helping by opening those doors and some of the windows so the place will air out? It's really nice here at night. But if you're hot or if you get hot, we can turn on the air conditioner.

"I'm fine, actually I bet it's going to be really nice."

Once she uncovered the sofa and chairs, she stood holding the sheets in her hands. "I'll put the place in order tomorrow. Just remember we have nothing for breakfast in the morning. The bedrooms are this way. I just can't do anything else."

Once she entered her bedroom, she dropped the sheets on the floor of her room. It was like the bed was just calling her name. Jynx started peeling off her wet clothes, leaving them lay wherever they landed. Personally she didn't care. She was sore and exhausted. All she wanted was to sleep and to be safe.

Jynx walked up to the bed and pulled the covers down and crawled in. "This is heaven." Instant contentment made her toes curl as she stretched out.

She watched as Stone removed his jeans and stood next to the bed, watching her. She felt shivers down her spine. He was so perfect. Her heart quickened and her breasts tightened in response. As tired as she was, her body responded to his gorgeous physique. He was solid and full of rippled muscles. Jynx loved what he represented: strength, solidity, someone she could trust.

When he climbed in next to her, Stone pulled her into the curve of his body to spoon and she went willingly. The sigh escaped as pleasure filled her. Jynx leaned towards him in the darkness of the room. "Thank you for being here with me."

There were no words needed between the them as Stone pulled her into his body, making her feel safe. Her eyelids closed and sleep claimed her.

* * *

Jynx's eyes snapped opened when her internal alarm jerked her awake, filling her with apprehension. Her stomach clenched as the hairs on the back of her neck stood on end. Something was not right. Before her conscious could register what was happening, a hand covered her mouth cutting off any sound.

With a swiftness and strength for pure survival, she grasped the hand covering her mouth and twisted, adding enough pressure to break the arm. At the same time she rolled from under the covers. It happened so fast, Jynx's heart raced in her ears.

"Jynx! It's me, Milla." She whimpered with pain.

"Milla?" Jynx released her quickly, realizing the woman standing before her who was now holding her arm against her chest was a ghost. Jynx had made her that way to keep her safe. "What are you doing here?" A thousand questions surfaced, and fear. Not for herself but for the woman standing before her.

"You're not safe with me," Jynx urged.

Filled with dread she turned towards Stone. How was she going to explain without telling him everything? More lies. They were piling up.

"You don't have to worry about him. He'll sleep for a while. I needed to talk to you so I made sure we wouldn't be interrupted."

"You drugged him?" Jynx's anger surfaced.

"Nothing harmful, just a light sedative to make him sleep so we can talk. So, you're sweet on him?"

Jynx pinched the bridge of her nose and closed her eyes in distress. "Let's go into the kitchen, and I'll make us some coffee. I rather not discuss things in front of Stone." Jynx guided her towards the door.

"Maria is here, and Sal went to the store and picked up some stuff to prepare the house for you. I gave them a call while you were sleeping; Sal already knew you were here. You know they miss you and worry about you even more." Milla told her without batting an eye. "Come on. I'm hungry. I haven't had Mamma's cooking in a long time."

"You called them? You can't be here, Milla. I did illegal things to keep you away from your father. Faked your death. Gave you a new life. You are jeopardizing everything." Jynx hissed, feeling like she'd lost control of her life and the whole situation.

"You're not telling me anything I don't already know. I saw the news. I also know he tried to have you killed, and I won't stand by and allow that to happen. I'm not a scared young kid anymore. You have no clue what I can do now. The military made me into a human weapon. No one will hurt you. Not on my watch."

"Do you hear yourself? You're not on base with a team at your side. You have only me for backup. He'll kill us both, and it won't be pretty. He'll make us suffer, especially if he figures out who you are and that I plotted against him. There'll be no stopping your father."

"Do you think I'm stupid or something?"

"You're not listening to me," Jynx hissed.

"Yes, I am, but in my eyes you're my sister, family. My mother is in the kitchen while my father is out getting supplies. My birth mother was murdered because she wanted to divorce my father. When she tried to leave, he stopped her. I was only seven years old. I remember it every time I close my eyes. So you can get mad; I really don't care. I'm not going anywhere until I know you're safe and my so-called father is behind bars or dead. Does he know your identity yet or about sleeping beauty over there?"

"What am I going to do with you?" Jynx shook her head. "No. He's trying to hurt Merrick though Jynx."

"We need to stop him before he does, or hurts you or your witness," Milla explained.

"I see you have been keeping tabs on me. I've been thinking about it. There's no use putting your father behind bars. Not to mention the fact he has plenty of turncoats on his payroll. Gambino's so powerful he'll run things from the jail. Instead we need to cripple his cartel, ruin him." Her voice went down to a whisper when she spotted Maria turning towards them from the kitchen bar. The delicious aroma of food drifted through the house and made her stomach growl.

"It's a glorious morning when I have my two girls together." Maria's voice sounded like she was holding back tears. She held the kitchen dish towel against her chest as they approached. Jynx noticed how she had aged and over the years she seemed to have gotten shorter.

Jynx watched Milla run and throw her arms around Maria's neck.

"Mamma!" Milla excitedly exclaimed.

The best thing I ever did was putting those two together. Jynx smiled, feeling the love move across the room. She missed this, the sense of family.

Movement at the oven behind Maria and Milla caught Jynx's attention, and when the person stood and turned, Jynx staggered in surprise. "Momma?"

"Merrick."

Jynx watched her mother move to stand in front of the other two women holding each other tightly, waiting.

She ran full speed until she stood facing her. "You really are here?" Her words were garbled as tears started to fall. Momma!" It was all Jynx could get out as she broke down sobbing. She was afraid to touch her as if she might disappear and this turn into a cruel dream.

Instead her mother pulled Jynx into her arms. After a few stunned moments, Jynx raised her arms hesitantly around her mom. Her hand opened against her back to pull her closer. "Oh, Momma!" she whispered. It was everything she craved.

She could feel her mom's quiet sobbing against her neck. It only made Jynx sob harder. Jynx pulled back and ran the backs of her fingers across her cheek. "Please don't cry."

"These are happy tears, baby. It's been too long," Her mother explained.

"Mine, too, and a lot of stress. It's been ten years. Too long, but it's important to keep you safe. Mom," Jynx confessed. She turned to Milla. "Is this your doing?"

"Yes. You needed to see her. To remember why you keep doing what you do. Above all you needed to see her. Feel her love wrap around you and make you remember how much you love your family. And more so, that your family loves you," Milla quoted.

"But you put her in danger as well," Jynx reminded her.

"No, I haven't. I have taken precautions," Milla replied firmly. "You get to visit with her all day, and then I'll make sure she arrives home safely."

"But." Jynx started to argue.

"There are no buts. I did this for you. So stop fussing and enjoy the day with your mother, so I can do the same." Milla's confidence oozed from her.

"Hey, smarty pants, you're forgetting something." Jynx put her hands on her hips waiting for a response.

"For the love of god, what is it?" Milla's tone filled with annoyance.

"How do we explain my mother to Stone once he awakens from your drugging him?"

"We don't," Her mother cut in, putting her hands on her hips.

"I'm just part of the help. A neighbor helping out." Her mother shrugged. "We got this, Jynx." Her mother threw in her nickname for emphasis.

Jynx's mother grabbed her by the arms.

"I'm not going to lose my daughter. You got it? That scumbag has dominated our lives for the past ten years, making us live in fear. It's time we stand up for ourselves. I don't want to live in seclusion anymore. Milla's been training me how to shoot. I'm pretty good if I say so myself."

Jynx jerked away from her mother's grasp to face off against Milla. "How dare you!" She invaded Milla's personal space and shoved her, seeing red. "Why would you do that? I don't want her with a gun. I was protecting her, and now she thinks she's Rambo!" She was losing control and that wasn't like her. For the past ten years she'd put away a lot of criminals and taken care of her mother without a glitch. She noticed the fleeting look of hurt cross Milla's face right before anger changed her features.

She stumbled backwards when Milla retaliated and shoved her. Jynx went in for the attack, having lost her patience. Before she could land a punch, Milla surprised her by grabbing her fist before it made contact. In slow motion Jynx lost her balance when Milla flipped her over her shoulder, putting Jynx on her back. She looked up dazed. Milla still held her fist, with Jynx's arm stretched tight, and her foot was against her chest, pinned to the floor. "Say Uncle," Milla hissed.

Maria screamed for Sal in the background.

"Enough!" Her mother's command came from behind them. "You two will release one another and behave yourselves right now or else."

Like a child being fussed at after a fight, Jynx wanted to stick out her tongue at Milla in rebellion, but instead gave her a sheepish look. Jynx released Milla's ankle, opening her hands in surrender. Displaying obedience to her mother's outrage. Her arm was released and Milla's foot was removed from Jynx's chest. Before she could move, Milla offered her hand to help her up.

Begrudgingly she allowed Milla to help her stand and stood awkwardly next to Milla. She was not used to being reprimanded like a child, having been alone for so long, but her mother's stern command demanded compliance.

"You two look like two naughty children standing before their parent after having misbehaved." Her mother laughed. "Come on you two, make up. You know you want to."

"What's going on in here?" Sal came through the back door.

Milla rubbed her shoulder against Jynx's and smiled impishly. "Alright already." Jynx anger slowly sizzled out. "I'm sorry, but I still don't have to like what you've done."

"Well, before you forgive me, mm,.. I also put her through some self-defense classes." Milla visibly flinched, shut her eyes, and waited.

"Why? I don't understand your methods."
Defiantly Jynx crossed her arms. "You're not
forgiven." Anger flared, burning her insides
to the point she wanted to hurt Milla as if
she were a stranger. She was putting Jynx's
mother in danger. And she forbid it.

Fusion came into the kitchen having
heard the commotion, yawning like a real
feline.

"Listen, Jynx. I prepared your mother to
handle any situation. She needs to know how to
defend herself at all times. You're not around
her around the clock to protect her, if my
father ever figure things out and sends any of
his dumb goons to mess with her. I know and
you should know that your mother can defend
and take care of herself."

Jynx watched her as she motioned around
the room.

"This is my family. You, your mother
Pauline and Maria and Sal. I will protect them
with my last breath. But they also need to
know how to protect themselves in case of
emergency."

Jynx couldn't argue with her logic. She
watched Milla take her hand and lay it against
her own chest. She could feel Milla's
heartbeat racing under her fingertips.

"Don't be angry because I'm trying to
protect them the only way I know how."

Jynx put her forehead against Milla's as
she pulled her against her wrapping her arms
around her. "I get it, I get it, really I do.
I'm truly sorry. I should have known better,
but I've been caring for my momma for a long
time alone. I'm not used to sharing. And for
the record, I love you, too."

"Y'all need to come and eat before the
rain gets here." Sal shook his head. "I'm glad
to see you two made up. You're never too old
to get my belt" Sal gave Jynx a wink before he
grabbed a basket of hot biscuits and carried
them to the porch.

"Help carry the dishes outside before
the food gets cold." Maria motioned with her

hands. The bench style table held covered bowls of eggs, bacon, sausage, and pancakes with all the fixings.

Everyone found their spot around the table, talking all at once to each other. Jynx watched her family and neighbors come together and realized how much she needed each and everyone one of them. The love racing through her veins smothered her with pride, and such a deep sense of roots. She had to fix this mess without them getting hurt. The thing is Milla knew what she needed even though she hadn't talked with her in months. *The little shit*.

The clouds were moving in fast, looking dark and heavy. Jynx could smell the rain in the air from the slight breeze off Lake St. Catherine, making it pleasant. The way it looked, it wouldn't be long before the storm reached them. Sal was pouring coffee in her cup when she heard her mother's voice behind her.

"Well good morning." Jynx heard her say. "I'm Pauline, the lady over there is Maria, and that's her husband Sal. I'm Maria's sister."

Jynx turned toward the French doors to find Stone standing there, taking everything in while he searched the crowd. When their eyes met, Jynx could see questions there, the weariness in his eyes, his posture on the defensive.

The sound of her mother's voice pulled his attention back toward Jynx's mother, and Jynx watched him answer her politely.

"I'm Stone. I take it you already knew that." He sent a questioning look towards Jynx.

"They're my neighbors who watch over my place. Newton called them to tell them we were here and we needed supplies." She guided her glance towards Maria. "She spoils me."

"She starves herself," Maria scolded.

"Come, eat and tell us about yourself," Maria coached.

When Jynx turned to introduce Milla, she was no where in sight. Her plate was gone as well. All evidence of Milla ever being at the table had vanished. Jynx looked around searching for her, but she was gone.

She noticed Sal looking pointedly at her. Then he winked directing her glance towards the house. Jynx nodded once to confirm she understood. Hurriedly she glanced towards Stone to see if he noticed, but her mother held his attention.

Jynx hated that Milla had left to hide, but she understood as well. So many secrets, so many lies stacked on top of each other. One almost needed a dictionary to keep up to code. But it was her life. Fighting the heavy hitter crime-lords held a price. Now the price was too high, and the people she loved could be in danger. She had to stop the madness.

Without his noticing, she watched Stone with her mother. What it would be like to have him as her husband, to be a family. The thought entered her mind without warning, and she hurriedly discarded it. Once he figured out she had lied to him, he'd hate her with pure righteousness. The thing was she would deserve it because she couldn't tell him the truth.

It didn't stop her heart from slamming against her ribs at the sight of him. Her palms sweated, and her body ached with a fierce need she couldn't control. It was more than lust. Jynx had never expected to fall for him. With her last breath she would protect him.

None of it was his fault. It was hers and hers alone. Jynx held her cup to her lips and took a sip, watching her family. Suddenly she couldn't breathe. The smell of breakfast made her feel green. She stood up, pushing her chair back. She grabbed a biscuit and raised it to keep them from protesting. The weight of her burdens made her feet feel like lead as she walked down to the wharf, needing a moment to collect herself. Her eyes automatically went to the huge building between her house and Sal's. It was the gym she grew up in. Many boxing matches she had won and lost over the years. After her father had been killed she had locked it up. There were just too many memories. Tears burned behind her eyes with the thought. Being home was a double-edged sword, not to mention her mother being here. How she had missed her mother!

The breeze came off the water, whipping at her hair and clothes. Peace and quietness soothed her like nothing else could. This was why she came here. It was always the reason she returned. The tranquilly helped her frazzled nerves. Like now.

For miles all she could see was marsh and water. It was raining in the distance heading her way. She stood at the edge of the dock, curling her toes, leaning against a wooden piling, staring ahead while she waited. A small boat with two people caught her attention. As she watched them, she noticed neither one was fishing. Jynx set her cup on the piling and threw pieces of the biscuit in the water while she secretly watched them.

The fish came and quickly pulled the their breakfast under the water. The boat bobbed up and down, and Jynx realized the two in the boat had to be Milla's people, military. With hand signals she released them from their watch. They needed to be on land before the storm set in.

The first drop of rain fell into her coffee cup. It didn't matter anyhow, what remained in the cup had turned cold. Another raindrop fell and more followed. It was what she had been waiting for, the cleansing of her soul. Jynx allowed the rain to drench her. She tilted her face to the sky, her arms went out on each side of her body.

The stress overwhelmed her to the point of losing herself. The tears finally slipped down her cheeks. Slow at first but once she started they took control and she went to her knees feeling broken. This situation had blown out of proportion, and Jynx needed to put out the fire before she lost everything she had worked for to keep her mother and the people she loved safe.

Right now she needed mercy against the bad karma plaguing her. There were only a few times she permitted herself to fall apart but it seemed recently she'd cried more than ever. It was so unfair! After all these years she had found love. He sort of reminded her of her father. More importantly she knew her father would have given his approval. But in the end, after the lies, Jynx/Merrick had destroyed any chance at happiness even before it really started. She cried harder.

The hand on her shoulder made her scream. "No!" Automatically in defense her body whirled around and started to fall backwards into the water. As she was falling in what seemed like slow motion, Jynx realized her "attacker" was Sal. She frantically scrambled to grab onto something before she went tumbling into the water. Sal grabbed her and pulled her into his arms, preventing her from an undignified swim. Jynx held fast, feeling thankful.

"I gotcha, honey," Sal said against her ear.

Sal had a quiet dignity about him, older. He always made her feel safe, but it wasn't just that. It was the power of his confidence. It made her wonder what he was all about. He carried a gun, and he made sure she and his neighbors were safe. She smiled a secret smile. Sal was the neighborhood watch all by himself.

Since her father had died, Sal was the only father figure she knew. "I'm sorry. You just caught me off guard." Jynx released her hold on his shoulders.

"Don't be silly. You have a lot on your plate. Whenever you're here, I know you're at your worse. It's the only time you come. To recharge yourself."

"How do you know?" Jynx looked surprised.

"Merrick, darling." His fingers went under her chin to make her look at him. "I've known you all your life. Your father and I were best friends. I know you probably better than you know yourself."

A streak of lightning raced across the sky, catching her attention. It was immediately followed by a roar of thunder, vibrating the ground under their feet. "Come on. Let's get off the dock before we get struck by lightning. Jynx grabbed his hand and ran towards the huge garage not far off.

Once inside Jynx turned on the lights and went straight to the bathroom to look for towels. A small closet held clothes for when she was hold up in here working so she could change if there was a need.

"You go first, Pops. I'll wait for you to get warmed up. While you're in, I'll take a look around." Jynx noticed for the first time how old he was getting and that worried her. To her, he was Jynx's superman. Sometimes she thought she lived in a damn bubble. "Go on, I'll be right behind you when your finished." Jynx turned away from him, feeling her eyes burn. "Damn crybaby!" she mumbled, disgusted with herself.

That's when she saw it. Tears gathered in her eyes. "It's the Aquarius!" Jynx whispered.

Chapter 8

The greatest invention she had ever
designed sat in front of her. *The Aquarius!*
Well, that's what she had decided to call her.
After going to the aquarium as a young girl,
she dreamed about being underwater. Throughout
the years she found herself thinking of this.
As a young girl, she drew her ideas as they
came to her. Her journal was huge, filled with
floor plans, ideas, and notes to self.

One day, Jynx had shared her journal
with Sal after he questioned her about what
she was writing. His excitement and approval
encouraged her go out and buy an old submarine
that she had located at a private auction.
From her designs Sal cut the old submarine she
had bought. literally in half, but not before
salvaging some of the insides and saving them
to reuse on the *Aquarius*. Jynx designed her
ideas on paper using part of a sub, but she
wanted it bigger to hold a lot of people, like
the famous *Nautilus* except more elaborate.

"I hired a small crew," Sal spoke behind
her making her jump.

"It's really coming together." She
turned to look at him. "It's all because of
you. I don't know what to say." Instead she
hugged him. "Thank you."

"Go get changed before you get sick."

Jynx smiled. He always fussed over her,
making her feel loved and wanted. It dawned on
her suddenly that she couldn't sit around and
wait any longer. The stress, the what-ifs, it
was all making her more than a little crazy.
She was starting to worry how long she could
keep her secrets, and her family safe. The
stress was making her shoulders and neck hurt.
A weak voice in her mind whispered that she
was a failure. Another stronger part of her
denied it, making her straighten her spine.
Jynx looked over her shoulder at Sal. He stood
there watching her as she closed the bathroom
door. This had to end now. She had never
allowed things to escalate to this scale
before. For the first time ever things had

gotten way out of control and it was up to her to stop Gambino.

When she looked at her reflection in the bathroom mirror, Jynx hardly recognized the wild-eyed woman staring back at her. The more she stared at herself the more she couldn't see. Jynx shook her head, dispelling the negative feelings that were consuming her. "Now or never!" Her voice sounded strong and determined. She reached into the closet and pulled out a pair of black pants and a shirt.

It only took her a few minutes in the shower, allowing the hot water to wash away the last remaining feelings of weakness and failure. When she stepped out, she had a plan. Moments later, she was dressed and mentally preparing herself as she flipped the switches of the fuse box, plunging the whole place in darkness. She only had a few moments before the emergency generator came on.

She paused next to Sal without a word. Jynx stood close to him, watching him fumble in the dark.

"Damn. I knew it! I shouldn't have let her out of my sight. Damn, damn, damn!"

He was angry with himself Jnyx realized. He brushed up against her in a feather light touch. Jynx held her breath to see if he noticed. Part of her wanted to tell him how much she loved him, that she was going to make it all better, that it wasn't his fault and not to be angry or upset with himself. In the end she refrained from saying anything.

Jynx couldn't think about what Stone would think. *He's safe with Sal as his bodyguard.* She needed some breathing space to think straight and prepare herself for the heartbreak that was to come, when this was over. How could she really expect anything different? Everything was a lie except for the fact she had fallen in love with him. She'd die before she would allow Gambino and his thugs get to him. Jynx wanted to scream, hit and just be pissed off but instead she held it in for when she needed that hate to help her defeat her enemy.

It just made her more determined to fix this mess. *How am I going to fix this?* She wondered, but deep down she knew. She'd have to kill Gambino. It was the only way to keep him from hurting her family. He had gotten too close and knew too much now, but before she did it, Jynx needed to go back to her place as Merrick and see exactly what he really knew and how many others were in the know. She would need to take them down to keep her family out of their clutches, so she need weapons and ammo and she knew just where to get them.

When she slipped outside, it was raining so hard she couldn't see anything. It wasn't nighttime, but the darkness from the heavy rain clouds made it easy for her to slip off into the water. Jynx knew these waters like the back of her hand, and she knew the risk of encountering an alligator or a snake, but hope that wouldn't happen. She swam out and down the canal, swimming past the extra lot with the Gym her father built with Sal. It's been locked up for years. In the old days when they opened the doors the alarm would sound allowing the kids around a safe place. They would come and box each other with Sal and her father as referee**s**. Now it was a painful reminder.

Sal's house was huge, beautiful her second home a safe place filled with love, but she kept swimming until she was far from the people she loved. When she finally made it far enough, Jynx pulled herself out behind a small boat launch.

Jynx waited, standing in the shadows and watching the area for any signs of movement. When she knew it was clear, she started to jog in the shadows away from the street and passersby. After almost two hours of jogging and walking fast, she finally stopped. Hidden in a tree line she waited until she caught her breath.

The parking lot of the Ten Pin Bowling Alley was packed, especially considering the weather. It was the only place to have some fun for the young and old out this way. About ten years ago Jynx had bought the run-down place. It took quite a chunk of money but she had given it a facelift, added two sets of 3-D virtual pods and a small paint ball arena. Since then it had really made its money back.

At the back of the building she had created a small storage space set among the walls of the back of the building. That way she didn't have to go inside where people would see her. It was a genius idea. The entrance was hidden from being noticed. When she had put new walls up, she had set them up flush, and the door only opened by facial recognition. The outside light was the camera.

The door opened immediately and a light came on inside. The door closed slowly behind her. It was only the size of a ten by ten but that was all she needed for a small sofa and a loft with a mattress. A college refrigerator filled out only bottled water sat under a small corner counter space with a small sink for washing dishes and a microwave. In the cabinet above the sink were a few cans of soup and fruit. Her stomach growled.

On the other side was the door to a very small bathroom with only a shower stall and toilet. On the door itself hung a full-length mirror. Her mind went to Stone, and she didn't want to think about how much she missed having him around. Jynx loved the way he looked at her. It made her shiver with just the memory, and all she'd have at the end of all this was only the memory. The way he touched her and kissed her was like they were the only two beings in the universe.

Jynx stripped out of her wet clothes and hung them on hangers to dry. She changed into some dry undies and made herself a cup of hot tea. At this location there was no Internet, no phone. It was a primitive location for safety reasons. Not even Newton and Fusion would be able to find her at this site. She felt the weight of the world on her shoulders, but there was a way to fix it. Jynx just needed to find out the right way.

After the tea, which seemed to calm her, she climbed the ladder to the loft for a nap. She wanted to be prepared for what was to come. At the top far end behind the pillows was a safe. She opened it and pulled out a Smith & Wesson forty-five. The only thing left inside was some cash and a set of keys.

All she wanted was an hour to rest so her mind could be clear and focused on her plan. She realized once she was home Gambino would come to her. Jynx just wondered how long would that take.

She tried to close her eyes and relax. It was moments like this when she wished her father was here more than ever before. He had been good at what he did. It was why Gambino had him killed. She set the alarm on her watch and made herself close her eyes. Jynx tossed and turned, grumbling under her breath but all she could do was just lie there and look at the ceiling.

A small lamp sat on top of the safe. She reached over to turn it on. A forgotten book caught her attention. Maybe she would get sleepy if she read for a little while.

Startled from a dead sleep Jynx bolted upright, heart pounding, and the taste of fear on her tongue as the alarm rang on her watch. "Shit!" Jynx fumed. *What a way to wake up! So much for feeling rested!*

She fell back against the pillows and covered her eyes with the back of her arm. The nap was supposed to make her feel rested but dreaming of Stone only made her feel lonely and needy.

"Alright!" She berated herself out loud. "Time to get the show on the road." Jynx climbed down the ladder and picked out a causal dressy suit. Classic navy slacks, a cream blouse, and a matching navy blazer. Her hair was the hardest, especially because her dreads were still wet. She added the wig and double secured it in place, just in case Gambino tried to put his grimy fingers in it.

She did her makeup as usual for a day at the office. Before she added mascara she slipped her contacts in, changing her eye color back to brown. Jynx loved how she could transform everything about herself to keep the real her secret. The last thing she needed was her shoes. Jynx found a pair of flats at the back of her closet. At this time practical was more important than...

Before she left, she washed her teacup and grabbed the set of keys and her gun from the safe. At the last moment she threw the covers over the mattress. After everything was back in place, she used the indoor remote to open the door. The rain had finally slowed down to a drizzle. Once she was outside the door closed behind her, locking automatically. She walked away from the business without being noticed. Once again she was Merrick Hardin. After she was far enough away she found a teenager and asked to use her phone for a hundred dollars.

She called a taxi service to come pick her up. She ended up having to wait for about thirty minutes before the cabby pulled up.

"You're the lady waiting for a cab?"

The woman behind the wheel had scarlet red hair in pigtails with freckles spread across her nose and cheeks, the bluest eyes Merrick had ever seen, and a huge smile revealing braces. "Yes, that would be me."

"Sorry for your wait. I had some rich old dude, drunk off his keister, who couldn't remember where he lived. Then he kept calling me Pippy Longstockings. The nerve of the bastard!"

The stress and worry making her feel exhausted caused Merrick to burst out laughing. "I'm sorry. Really." But another wave of hysteria hit her when she glanced at the girl. Merrick put her hand out to signal to wait. "Don't leave me." She bent over at the waist trying to catch her breath. "I'm sorry, really." Merrick breathed between giggles. "Have you looked at yourself in a mirror lately? Honestly?" Another burst of laughter erupted.

The girl behind the wheel started to smile but she was fighting the urge. A chuckle came out against her will, then another, until she too started laugh. They both were laughing. "I have to get out of here." Merrick opened the back door, falling into the cab with tears in her eyes from laughing. They were both still giggling as she shut the door. Out the corner of her eye she saw Sal's truck approaching. The laughter was gone, and Jynx threw herself down to the floorboards to hide.

"Holy Crap!" the driver blurted.

The car shot off, throwing rocks as the cab fishtailed. The cab threw Merrick around like a sack of potatoes. "Ouch!" she yelped when her head hit the door. The driver wasn't laughing any longer either as she took off like a bat out of hell. Merrick stayed down just in case Sal noticed her.

After a few minutes the driver said, "All's clear. You can get up now."

"Thank you," Merrick said, rubbing her head and dusting off her outfit with the other hand.

"Are you in some kind of trouble? Do we need to call the cops?"

"No. I'm okay. Could you drop me off at a car rental place, please?"

"Yeah, no problem. I didn't mean to pry."

"I didn't think you were. Actually I think you were very sweet for being so protective over me. I thank you for that," Merrick commented. It was only a short drive until she pulled up at a place to rent cars.

"I'll wait here just in case you can't find anything you want to rent, or if their rates are too high," the cabby announced.

"Wait!" the cab driver screamed to get her attention.

Merrick looked through the open car door. "Yes?"

"You know, lady, I could just drive you wherever you need to go. That way you could just pay me."

Merrick put her head down to collect her thoughts. "Where I'm going probably will be a one way trip. So it'll be safer for all concerned if I rent a car. You, I can't replace. Nor could I see putting you in danger, but thank you all the same." Merrick shut the door ending the conversation.

"Wait!"

Merrick turned around, feeling more than a little impatient at seeing the young driver standing in the doorway looking over the top of the cab.

"You can rent a car all you want, but I'm just going to follow you. Someone has to be your backup, lady."

"You need to leave, right now, and forget you ever saw me." When there was no response, Merrick asked, "What's your problem anyway? You have a death wish or something?"

"If I die there is no one to stand over my grave, no one to shed a tear. But when I look at you, I can see you have a family. You're alone for whatever reason. I've lived on the streets for as long as I can remember. When I look at someone, I can tell if that person needs help, and you lady, you need help."

In the middle of the parking lot of the rental place, Merrick watched the driver get back behind the wheel and shut the door.

"May I help you?" Obviously one of her employee's trying to assistant her. Still, Merrick just stood there unsure of what to do. Merrick glanced over her shoulder at the employee and back to the cab where she could see Pippy watching her waiting.

Again she turned halfway to the employee. "No, thanks, I have a ride." Merrick took a step towards the cab, dismissing the assistant. "It's your funeral."

After Merrick shut the door behind her and she was firmly seated, the cabby stomped on the gas pedal causing the tires to smoke. The cab just missed a parked car.

"Where're we headed?"

"My house off of City Park. You can park down the street so you're not seen."

Without warning the cab swerved to the side of the road as Pippy slammed on the brakes. Merrick grabbed the back of the wire mesh separating the driver of the cab and held on for dear life. "What the hell?" Merrick hissed. She watched the girl turn to look at her.

"Look, I'm twenty-five. My mother was a cocaine addict, and I lived on the streets with her. When I was eighteen, I literally fell into the recruiting office, starving, homeless, and begging for them to accept me into the military. I didn't want to end up like my mother."

I have experience. I'm on leave, but I can help. I'm not sure what's going on, but I'm not letting you out of my sight. Got it, lady?"

"Ok, Pippy! You win. You can drive a few more blocks and then turn right. It's the second house on the right.

"You can't miss it. Do you have a piece of paper and pen?" After Pippy gave her the pencil, Merrick wrote her note. "If I don't make it I want you to get in touch with Sal Rantza, his phone number is on the paper." Merrick shoved the paper back to her through the opening, waiting for her to grab it. When she did Merrick watched her. The girl didn't even look at the paper before she shoved it into the ashtray.

"Sure thing."

They turned the curb, but Merrick was looking around for anything unusual, like a car that didn't belong. Usually she'd have Newton or Fusion scan the area, but she had left them behind. She'd have to do it herself.

Well, except for girl, G.i.Jane. *She didn't know how things were going to work with having her with her, but she was glad she wasn't by herself.* Although if the girl thought for one moment that she was going to allow her get into any kind of trouble, she'd better think again.

"What the hell is going on?"

Merrick heard the cabby, but she was taking in the scene while the driver slowed down in front of her house where yellow tape was everywhere. At one window a shutter hung lopsided from its secured hinge. A few broken windows with jagged edges made her home look dangerous. The lawn was littered with debris. Merrick had no idea where it came from. When the cab stopped, Pippy glanced over her shoulder giving her a hard look.

"Tell me this isn't your house."

"I wish I could." Merrick replied, feeling a lump in her throat. She loved her home. At least from what she could tell the basement was still intact.

"You better think again if you think I'm fucking letting you out of my cab."

The woman driver turned back around and hit the gas pedal so hard Merrick was thrown against the back of the seat. "What the hell are you doing? You have to go back." Merrick's anger surfaced.

Suddenly the tires squealed and smoke rose behind the car as Pippy slammed on the brakes.

Merrick tried to stop her body from slamming against the plastic partition, but her body slid off the seat without grace. Her hands shot out against the plastic to absorb the force of the impact. Still she couldn't stop the scream that forced it way past her lips.

"What is your problem? Damn it, you're going to kill me before the bad guys can," Merrick hissed.

Pippy turned towards her. "What the hell happened at your place and don't leave anything out."

"Look, I can't tell you shit so you can either take me back or let me out here. Then you can go on your merry way," Merrick announced feeling annoyed.

The cab sped backwards at a high rate of speed only to skid to a halt in front of Merrick's home. "Thanks!" Merrick threw money through the hole. "That should cover it." Before she could open the door, the car burst forward again throwing her back against the seat.

"What are you doing, you crazy bitch?" Merrick fumed.

"Look, I'm sorry for the rough ride, but you can't go in there half cocked. You need a plan of action, or you'll end up dead. In the military we don't do anything unless we plan out our attack. That way there is fewer causalities."

"Yes, well, there is no plan. I have to allow them to take me so I can find out what they know. It's as simple as that." Merrick tried not to go off on the girl, knowing she was only trying to look out for her.

"Well that shit isn't going to fly, sweetheart. You have to have a rescue mission in place."

"You're as subtle as a freight train the way you're driving up and down the street. You might as well put a bull's-eye on us." Merrick declared indignantly.

"Okay, okay, I'll make the block and stop. So, are you going to tell me what we're up against at least?"

"You really want to know?" Merrick gave her a disgusted look.

"Yes."

"Joseph Gambino." It was all Merrick needed to say.

"Mother freaker!" Pippy whistled. "By some small miracle, do you know how to hold or even shoot a gun? Because, lady, we're not walking into a place that looks like it was destroyed by terrorists."

"The miracle is real. Not only can I hold a gun, I am a expert shot. And I can also fight." Merrick snapped.

"Ok, so this is the plan. We'll go in. I have some forgotten luggage in the trunk. I'll carry it inside for you, so we can check things out. They won't expect anything military by the looks of me, so I'm your biggest surprise."

While Pippy pulled up in the driveway breaking the yellow tape crossing over the drive, Merrick looked around trying to see what was different. It was hard to tell since everything was in a shambles. When the car stopped, Pippy jumped out and slid over the hood of the car to open Merrick's door. "This door sticks with the humidity."

"Thank you for the cab ride. Can you bring the luggage inside for me?" Merrick asked while she searched in her pocket for the keys. The trash cans were laying on their sides and garbage was everywhere. It actually looked like someone had gone through the trash. It was probably one of Gambino's men.

The sound of the suitcase dragging on the cement made Merrick turn to glance her way. Merrick could only smile at the picture Pippy painted of a weakened petite woman tugging on a heavy suitcase.

Merrick pulled the tape off the doorframe and inserted the key. The screen door was missing, and the wooden door was severely damaged. She would have to hire repairmen and a yard person to come take care of this mess. It was just too much for her to do by herself, but that was later, if she was still alive.

As she pushed open the door and walked in, the hairs on the back of her neck stood on end. Someone had either been there or was still there waiting to pounce.

Behind her Pippy the cabby dragged the heavy suitcase through the door backwards looking out the door, huffing and puffing for good measure. Merrick had to hand it to her, she was playing the part to the hilt.

Merrick walked through leaving Pippy in the main room.

"What happened here?" the nosy cabby asked.

"I woke up this morning, and I was out of coffee."

"I hardly believe you did this because you're out of coffee. Where do you want me to put this suitcase, ma'am?"

"If you don't mind, I rather not leave it in the living room. Just watch where you step and let's see what the bedroom looks like." Merrick started off toward the back of the house.

Her room looked as bad as the living room. It was more than being messy. Somebody had gone through her stuff searching for something. At least Merrick knew that whatever they were looking for they didn't find anything.

Her bedroom was trashed there was no other way to explain it. The dresser drawers were pulled out with her belongings thrown on the floor. Her bed was upside down, and it appeared that someone had used a chainsaw to cut the box spring in half. On one of the walls someone had had created graffiti art with spray cans which were thrown on the floor.

"You should call the police, ma'am. It looks like vandals broke into your house."

"You might as well leave the luggage in the door. It seems they didn't miss any of the rooms. I'm going to go check the kitchen."

"Don't leave me here by myself."

Merrick walked with a slow pace examining each room, searching the shadows for movement.

"Your place gives me the creeps. It's not safe to be in here. Let's leave and call the police."

For good measure Pippy held on to the back of Merrick's shirt, standing tight against her backside as if she were really afraid. Merrick gave her credit. The girl could win an Oscar for the role she was playing, or was she? Was she really scared?

"You can go ahead and leave if you want to. I'll be okay," Merrick whispered. She didn't know why it came out like that but it did.

Rays of sunlight peeked through the curtains but there were so many shadows without the lights being on. Merrick would have turned them on, but she didn't want to alert anyone if someone was still in her house.

"I've been waiting for you."

A huge man grabbed Merrick's arms from behind. Instantly Merrick took a step back and head-butted him hard in the face.

The man yelled but didn't release her. Instead he spun her around and slapped her hard across the face. Her head jerked from the impact.

Pippy screamed and tried reaching for Merrick, but another of Gambino's men grabbed her.

Merrick fumbled backwards as a sudden explosion echoed off the walls. Suddenly she realized what had happened. Gambino had shot the guy who slapped her with a bullet to the forehead.

"Hello, Ladies," Gambino announced.

Chapter 9

When the front door burst opened Stone moved lightning fast, using his bulk to shield the women inside. He pointed his gun at the intruder. "State your purpose or die here tonight," Stone hissed.

"Don't shoot, son. It's just me."

Someone screamed from the kitchen area. "Please don't shoot him." Maria yelled. Off to the side Stone heard movement from the kitchen. A lantern flared to life, sending much needed light.

"I'm sorry, sir. I was only guarding the women." Stone looked behind him. "Where's Jynx?" Stone lowered his gun.

He quickly crowded Sal's personal space. "Don't lie to me either." *If Jynx isn't with him where the hell is she, and why did she leave me behind?* He had never wanted anyone so much or felt so protective over. Maybe it was because he couldn't save the Senator's wife when she was at the cafe', but damn, that would sit in his gut like rotten garbage until the day he died.

Jynx was complex, smart and talented. He could tell she had secrets, but who didn't. Trust didn't come easy for her, and he understood that because Stone had never trusted anyone. She was a mystery, a puzzle to unravel and Stone thought of her as his. No matter what happened he knew he didn't want to walk away.

He loved being in her company. She tried to protect him. A small, itty bitty, little woman. It warmed his heart where the military made him hard, mean and a killing machine. Stone had to admit he loved her dreads, which surprised him. He wondered what her hair looked like down. Whenever they're eyes accidentally connected, sparks flamed in his gut and making his protective nature surface. A few times he caught her looking at him and his heart pounded hard against his ribs as if he was out on a dangerous mission.

Sal gave him a look of authority, which made Stone take a step back. "She thinks she gave me the slip," Sal grinned.

The confidence that came off of Sal stamped him as military or government. Stone had to know. "I'm guessing you're military or some form of government. Now is the time for truths because someone has been trying to kill her. I don't understand why she'd take off like that." Stone paced back and forth then paused and turned towards Sal. "Did she take Fusion and Newton?"

"Not that I know of. It would have given her away."

"Damn! When I find her... and I'm going to find her... I'm going to beat her ass!" Stone fumed.

That made Sal laugh.

"By your having to ask you don't know her at all. Jynx is all about family. If she can help it, she'll move heaven and earth to keep us out of any kind of danger,. The only reason she came to this place was to clear her mind," Sal confessed.

Milla burst into the living room, rain pouring off of her forming puddles on the wooden floors. "She's gone. My girls lost her in the water."

Stone watched as she ran to the nearest closet and yanked it open. "Who are you?"

"I'm her sister."

"Milla, I want you to tell the girls to search the perimeter and make sure we don't have any unwanted guests and Mother, lock-down the house. I want you all out of here in five minutes. Stone, come with me."

"I'm coming with you," Milla demanded with determination, while pulling dry clothes from a bag.

"No, you're not. You're going to protect your mother and neighbor. Make the call and let's get moving," Sal commanded.

Stone watched Milla talk into a walkie-talkie then grab her clothes. He noticed how she turned her back to him so he couldn't see her face.

Stone heard Sal whistle with a short, low burst, and six giant black Schnauzers came from the darkness. They were at full alert and quickly surrounded Sal, baring their teeth and growling loudly, showing their aggression. The hairs on their backs were raised. At a command from Sal, the dogs stopped and sat in obedience.

"You never told me what branch?" Stone searched the man's face waiting for him to answer.

"Secret Service. The president was my detail. Not a word in front of the wife. She thinks I worked out of an office at Homeland Security. Leave it at that."

"Should we check the building that's locked up over by your place?" Stone asked as he shook his head in agreement while watching him use sign language with the dogs. Pulling one of Jynx's shirts from a pocket, Sal let the dogs sniff. Two took off running along the water's edge sniffing and running. The other two took off racing down the street. The last two sat patiently, their tails wagging.

The women came out in a rush of panic and nerves. "The house is locked. We're ready," Maria stated. Milla stood behind her, looking away so Stone couldn't see her features.

"The girls will see you home. When all is clear send Frances to me and you keep Chloe with you," Sal told his wife as he kissed her cheek.

"Ok, come back to me the same as you're leaving, not a scratch. If they harmed one hair on Jynx's head, let loose your wrath."

The neighbor fisted her hands in Sal's shirt, sobbing uncontrollably. "Ti Prego Di rimandarmi mai figlia."

Stone didn't understand what she said to Sal, but he hugged her tight until the woman turned into his wife's arms to cry. The dogs nudged the women gently until they walked close together Stone noticed.

"Come on. We need to catch up to the dogs," Sal said as he started to jog after the dogs. "I have a truck up the road, so we'll head out after the dogs pick up her scent."

"Where do you think she went? I hate to even think that she went to her house? If she does, she'll be a sitting duck." Stone whispered low because sounds carry long distances over water.

"Look over there. The dogs picked up on her scent." Sal announced.

Stone picked up the pace, sprinting to keep the dogs in sight. He thought he might have to wait for Sal to catch up, but the older man was keeping pace.

When they reached the boat launch, the dogs went wild and started to run in circles around the small building. Stone watched as they started off again, away from the street. "I'd swear Jynx has had some military training. Look how the dogs are following her trail; it's not against the street. She used her head."

"Yes, she did. When she turned eighteen, she enlisted into the Marines. She did six years or so. I don't remember exactly. She thought she was a burden to us, but she was our blessing. Maria and I couldn't have children. After her father passed, she came to live with us. She's been our pride and joy."

Stone followed beside Sal, running at a good pace until he pointed to a black pickup truck. Stone ran to the passenger side and jumped in as the truck pulled off.

They rode in pace with the dogs. It was hard to keep track of them in the dark, but every now and again they could see movement. At one point Sal lost them and had to pull over. Sal whistled through his opened window and one came to the road. After another signal, the dog took off at a run. Stone's nerves were on edge. He wanted to do something, not just sit on the passenger side and wait.

This fear burning in his gut was different than anything he'd ever experienced before. He was taking this personally. His anger was bursting for release. Stone wanted to man, mutilate. If he didn't reach her in time and they hurt her, God have mercy on their souls because hell was coming. He slammed his fist against the dashboard. "Damn!" Stone hissed.

"Now son, if you hit that any harder you're going to deploy the emergency air bag."

"This is taking too damn long. If someone has her, they better not harm a hair on that pretty little head or else they're going to pay. I need to find her before whoever is after her gets to her. For days they have been hot on our tail, like red beans on rice. This has got to come to an end."

"I have a tracker on her, but she's smart and if she changed clothes I may not be able to find her, so that's why I'm using the dogs," Sal explained.

"I swear if she's okay, I'm going to turn her over my knee old fashion style and spank that ass. I feel so fucking helpless."

"Imagine how we feel."

A loud thunk at the back of the truck caused Stone to turn around whipping his pistol out ready to shoot through the glass. Fusion hunched down with her face close to the glass of the cab. A horn blew next to his window, and Newton revealed himself for a second before going invisible again.

Stone smiled and shook his head. "I should have known. These two leave me speechless."

"Yes, they're a miracle for sure." Sal observed with feeling.

They drove for what seemed like hours before the dogs stopped at an old bowling alley. Fusion leaped off the back of the truck at a dead run, as Stone jumped out before the truck stopped completely. The dogs looped around to the back without going inside. They moved back and forth but couldn't find where she had gone. "I think the dogs lost her scent."

Newton materialized. "I scanned the area. There is a small apartment behind this wall."

"I'll go inside and see if I can get to it from inside the bowling alley," Sal interjected.

"You will not be able to enter from inside," Newton stated.

"How can you tell?" Stone asked. "I don't see a way to enter from here."

One of the dogs started to dig at the edge, trying to get indoors. Sal called him back, and Stone watched Sal replace the broken stones, leaving no evidence that someone was trying to get indoors.

"She must have used another method of entering. A remote maybe," Sal hinted.

"Is she inside, Newton?" Stone asked. There's no reason to try to get in if she's not here."

"She's not here, but the scent is fresh. Fusion find Jynx." Newton gave the order.

"Can you tell how long ago she was here?" Stone asked.

"Wait!" Newton demanded. "Someone, a young female, is in the front of this dwelling telling someone she made an easy score of a hundred dollars just by allowing some chic to use her phone. Maybe one of you could go question her."

"I'm on it." Stone was already on the move toward the corner of the building as he answered Newton. Whoever made the easy score was going to tell him everything he wanted to know.

Stone stopped before reaching the front, listening to the conversation so he could determine which person he needed question. She was maybe seventeen, eighteen at the most. *This was going to be easy* he thought.

"Hello, I'm looking for my girlfriend. She has black dreads, really beautiful. By any chance have you see her?" Stone put on the charm and smiled. Someone had once told him his dimples could melt ice. He even winked for good measure.

"Sorry, Buster. I haven't seen her. Go wink at someone who gives a shit."

That didn't go as planned, so he tried a different method. "She might be in trouble. Can you help me?"

"Look, mister, I don't know who you are, but she was out of breath and seemed like she was on the run, so I'm not telling you jack shit. For all I know, you're the reason she was running, so piss off."

Stone watched the young girl turn and stomp into the bowling alley without even giving him a chance. He couldn't be more proud of her for protecting the other woman even though they didn't know each other. Time was of the essence though, and Stone couldn't take the chance of not trying to talk to her again. He needed answers. "Excuse me, sweetheart. All I need to know is how long ago you talked to her."

"Eat shit and die, loser! If you follow me again I'll scream rape."

His hands shot up in surrender. "Look, I love this girl more than my own life." He stood there for a moment in shock. Stone couldn't believe he just blurted that out. The thing was, Stone realized, he meant every word and he needed this girl to believe him.

"There are some really bad people after us, and if I don't get to her first this could end in a bad way." To show he meant business he raised his shirt. "A couple of days ago someone shot me, and now they're after Jynx." Stone waited while she debated whether she believed him or not. He watched how she squirmed in indecision. It was there in the set of her jaw and the determined look in her eyes. She wasn't buying it.

"Time is of the essence. Please," Stone begged. He reached for the girl's hand and held it gently. "I really need to find her."

Finally, he saw when she changed her mind. He watched her pull out her cell phone and take his picture.

"I'll help you, but I want to see your driver's license, and if I find out that you hurt her, I'll report you. I swear I will."

Before he could take out his wallet from his pants pocket, the girl called a group of teenagers over.

"Take his picture, y'all. I want everyone to get a good look at him just in case I need backup."

One of the boys pulled her behind him. "Why would you need backup?" The teenager bucked up. The other boys stepped up beside him to show support.

"Dude, why don't you get to stepping and leave the girl alone before we call the cops." The main boy crossed his arms showing his defiance.

This was getting ridiculous. "Look, I'm not here to cause anyone any trouble. I'm losing valuable time here and a girl's life is at stake" Stone said with determination.

"What girl?" one of the boys asked.

Stone ran his hand through his hair, trying to stay calm. "Never mind. You're wasting time and I don't have it to lose." He turned and started to walk off.

"Wait! The lady called for a cab," the girl said.

Stone turned to her. "Do you know which company?"

"No, but she used my phone so the phone number is still in my phone."

Stone walked up to her as he pulled his wallet out and pulled out his driver's license and his military card. "Here, take a picture of both of my ID's." It didn't stop the boys from crowding her just to make sure she was safe from him.

The girl handed over her phone. It only took a moment to get the number before he handed it back to her. "Thank you, and I appreciate how you tried to protect Jynx. Now if anyone else shows up asking questions be careful. They're probably the bad guys. They won't care if you're kids. They will kill you without thinking twice."

"Is she going to be okay?" the girl asked, looking upset.

"If I have anything to do about it, yes, she'll be fine. I swear," Stone vowed, setting his hand on the girl's shoulder. The girl looked up with tears in her eyes.

"I'm sorry I didn't tell you right away. You see, my mom's boyfriend beats her. That's why I didn't want to say anything. We tried to leave, but he always finds us."

"Since you helped me, I promise I'll help you. First, I have to take care of this, but I swear on my honor, I'll be back for you and your mother." Stone squeezed her shoulder.

As he walked toward the doors, another girl whispered loud enough where he heard, You know he's not coming back, right?

That pissed him off. He turned. "That's where you're wrong, young lady. My promises mean something." *That's what's wrong with people today. People just don't step up to the plate when there is something bad happening.*

When he stepped outside, Sal was waiting for him sitting in his truck. The dogs were gone. Impatience shone all over his face.

"What took you so damn long?" Sal hissed.

"The kids were trying to protect Jynx and wouldn't give up any information. They even took a picture of my driver's license and military ID and threatened that if I hurt the girl, they'd report me." Stone smiled. "It was admirable. Where are the dogs?"

He dialed the number to the cab service and after talking to someone for a few minutes and going back and forth, Stone hung up. "Damn!" Stone swore.

"What? What did they say?" Sal demanded.

"The cab driver hasn't made it back yet," Stone replied.

"You know what that means, right?" Sal asked.

"Yeah. They're missing," Stone hissed. His stomach knotted up and he felt so damn helpless. "Time is running out. The cab supervisor is running the GPS on the car to see if they can find out its location. They're going to call right back, but said it might take a few minutes."

Sal took off, slamming his foot on the gas pedal and throwing Stone against the seat as the car served into traffic.

"We need to get to the cab company."

"No! That's out of our way. If we drive there, we might have to backtrack. We can't afford to lose anymore time. Let's head to the house and see what we can find. I think that is our best bet."

Stone's cell rang and he answered it before it could ring twice. "This is Command Sergeant Major Stone speaking." Stone shrugged towards Sal.

The cab supervisor called and gave him the address and said that the police had been called as well. "Thank you for the information." He hung up and looked at Sal. "Drive fast. We need to get to the house before the police show up. The cab's there."

Stone listened in as Sal pulled out his cell phone and made a call. He knew Sal was talking to Milla.

"Who's the girl?" Stone asked when he hung up. "And don't tell me nobody. She hid her face from me more than once. I want to know if she could be a leak."

"She's not a leak. I would stake my life on it."

The way he said it made Stone believe him. He turned towards Sal to get his full attention. "Then you might want to start filling me in, man. We need be able to trust each other when we go in there. The way it sounds she's coming even though you told her to stay put. I don't need any surprises." Stone slammed his fist against the dashboard." Jynx's life is at stake and I'm not having anyone put her in any more danger than she's already in just because you all were not up front with me."

Stone stared him down. He wasn't relenting because the only person that mattered to him was Jynx, and he didn't give a flying shit who else survived. "Look, I'm in love with Jynx, and I'm not going anywhere. I just thought you should start getting used to the idea."

"Oh, really? It's not my place to tell you anything, but what I will say is Jynx saved her life and put her in our family. Maria and I have raised her as our own since she was twelve."

"That's good enough for now. I just wanted to be able to trust her in a tight spot," Stone stated. "We need a plan of action. You know we can't just go busting in."

"Yes, I know. I think we can get Fusion in easy enough."

"Oh, yes!" Stone sounded excited for the first time." When I was riding Newton, he made us both invisible. I wonder if Fusion can do the same thing."

"Yes, I can get you in."

Stone's head whipped around to look at Fusion through the glass.

"Fusion blue-toothed his voice box through to the radio." Sal explained. "It's how we speak to each other without Newton around."

"Ingenious," Stone said with wonder in his voice. "How does Fusion know when to send his voice?"

"That, my friend, is up to Jynx to explain, not I."

Stone watched Sal shrug his shoulders as if they were talking about the weather. "You didn't know about the bowling alley, did you?"

"No, I didn't, but there are probably a lot of things that get by me nowadays. Old age does come with a price."

"I don't know what kind of bullshit you're throwing, but I'm not buying it. You might want to try a different angle," Stone laughed. "How much longer?"

"It shouldn't be too much longer. Maybe fifteen to twenty minutes."

"Tell me you're not serious. Your ass needs to stop driving like some little old lady and get there already. If something happens to Jynx because you're taking your time..." Stone bit his tongue to stop the angry flow of words.

"Newton is inside the house. There are about fifteen men total. Two of them are sitting in an unmarked car watching the street. Jynx and the woman are tied up. One of Jynx's eyes is swollen shut from one of the men slapping her in the face." Newton broadcasted over the radio.

"Do you know who touched Jynx?" Stone stormed, pulling his gun out and making sure a bullet was in the chamber. "Can we get there already?" Stone hissed.

Sal's phone rang, cutting off anything Stone might have added to his ranting. After a few words, Sal hung up the phone and looked over at him.

"That was Milla. She's coming from the other side. They're on foot easing down the street."

"You mean to tell that the women you told not to come beat us to her place? What the fuck is wrong with this picture?" Stone yelled.

"Look, you need to calm down. You can't go in there half-cocked or you'll get all of us killed while you're trying to be Rambo."

Before he could say anything, Sal pulled over and killed the engine. "Fusion is going to get us in, but we're waiting on the girls so we can all get in undetected."

"Fusion, are you ready?" Stone turned toward the cat through the back window. "Are you up for this, girl? Because if you're not or you find yourself in trouble, come to me so I can keep you safe. I can't let anything happen to you. I don't want Jynx to ever experience what happened earlier."

The steam punk jaguar cat jumped down next to Stone's door as the girls approached. Milla coached the girls to come together into a circle.

"Outside the house there is a black unmarked Suburban with two guys playing on their cell phones. Two at the door, and the rest are inside. The bad news is that Gambino himself is inside. All of them are armed," Milla warned.

Sal's cell phone went off again, interrupting the meeting.

"What the hell?" Stone yelled. "Get off the damn phone."

"Hold on." He put his finger over his mouth to shut Stone up.

Stone paced back and forth like a caged panther. When Sal shut his phone Stone was on him. He bunched his hands into Sal's shirt and shoved him against a tree.

"You son of a bitch! I should beat you right here and now!"

"Release me, Stone, or I'll put you on the ground. This isn't a pissing contest, so back off," Sal commanded.

"I have news. I don't know what's going on with the girls but it seems to me that girl isn't exactly a regular cab driver. It looks like she might have military training.

"Okay, lets go get Jynx," Stone commanded.

"Wait we can't go in there empty-handed." Sal, walked to the back of his truck and, using a remote, opened up the back of his truck. When the top raised, Sal jumped in and turned around "Come and pick your poison."

Stone swung his body over the side and stood next to Sal looking down as he clicked

the remote and shelves moved in and out until
another shelf replaced the other one and
different styles of guns were displayed along
with ammo.

"Hell, yeah!" Stone reached in and
pulled out a ankle knife and another knife for
his belt. He grabbed an M-16 and some extra
clips. A Glock went into a pocket with some
extra clips. Stone just grabbed what he could
carry and hide because there wasn't a gun he
couldn't shoot. When everyone was loaded and
ready, they approached the house with caution.

Chapter 10

"Run!" The cab driver pulled hard, propelling her forward only to collide into a tall tree trunk of a man. The force of the impact rocked Merrick backwards. He blocked their escape. He was so huge and the grin he sent Merrick curled her toes. They were in trouble. Big trouble.

Merrick unceremoniously fell into Pippy. Instead of acting afraid, Merrick quickly decided to play it off. "Relax, it's only Gambino. There is no need to be afraid, he's my client." Merrick peeled off Pippy's vise-like gripping fingers one by one from her skin and turned toward Gambino. She winked at Pippy secretly to play along. "What are you doing here? And why are you sitting in my house in the dark?"

"I've been waiting for you actually." Merrick felt movement behind Pippy, but she didn't turn around as the guy blocking their exit turned the light on, temporarily blinding Merrick.

"I was concerned that you were killed after watching the news about your being in a car accident, but when they couldn't find your body, I kind of figured I should come and check on my investment. To make sure my attorney was safe. When I arrived, your place was in a shambles so I decided to stick around. I was tailing your maid but she gave us the slip, so I've been waiting here. I also have a few people looking for you."

Merrick kept her courtroom face on, but inside she was seething. *The lair.* Mentally she shook off the anger. Before she spoke she cleared her voice making sure when she did speak her voice sounded normal. "Thank you for your concern, but as you can see I'm fine.

"Even though, I don't believe the wreck was an accident. Whoever was driving the truck was trying to kill me, so I decided to lay low, but I can't just hide, so I decided to come home. I also sent my maid on a vacation until I know it's safe for her to return."

Merrick laughed. "She's not going to like coming home to this." Merrick picked up one of her kitchen chairs from the floor and sat down. If she displayed fear in front of Gambino, she'd become one of his pawns.

"I had the guys pack up some of your personal belongings and sent them to my house. You can't stay here until your place is repaired, and you just informed me that you think someone is trying to kill you. Before you argue, it's just not safe for you here by yourself," Gambino stated.

"Excuse me? I'm not going to your place and that is a fact. Not to mention, I can't believe you had your men go through my personal belongings. Who gave you that right?" Merrick fumed stomping her foot. *How dare he try to man handle me!* She fumed indignantly.

"You don't have to get yourself in a huff, darling. I have a business opportunity that I feel is perfect for you and me."

"You and me?" Merrick's brain couldn't wrap her mind around the man's audacity. "So you have a business proposal?" Merrick questioned him flabbergasted at the nerve of his stupidity.

"Not here. After a hot shower at my place, and a steak dinner, we can discuss things while you relax. It appears that my little darling has had a rough few days." Gambino leisurely leaned forward allowing his finger to run under her chin.

Merrick had to force herself not to flinch. "First of all Gambino."

"Call me Joseph." Gambino cut in.

"Gambino, I'm not your darling." Merrick removed his hand from touching her, pushing his hand toward him in a show of defiance. "Ever!" Her tone was clear. "We do not have that kind of relationship nor do I plan on it," Merrick tossed the words at him with a raise of her chin. "You can stop trying to romance me because it's a lost cause." She watched the hurt flash in his eyes before he quickly hid it.

Gambino moved in fast, fisting his hand in her hair, jerking her head back making her look up at him. "No one tells me no, darling." He released her. "I'm trying to do this without treating you as I would someone else, anyone else for that matter, but you're making it difficult."

Out of the corner of Merrick's eye she saw Pippy move to intervene, but before she could make contact, two huge goons picked her up and jerked her backward. Merrick watched her struggle against the two, giving them hell she noticed.

"Don't let that asshole bully you!" Pippy yelled from across the room while struggling with her assailants.

"Contain her now!" Gambino hissed at the two men.

He leaned back in his chair and reached inside his jacket. "I think you're making a grave mistake. We could have been great together." Gambino shrugged as he pulled out a small flash drive from inside his coat. He tossed it at her.

Merrick let it fall to the floor. "Tell me what's on it."

"A list of people who are incarcerated in different parishes. I want them out and I want you to make that happen."

She leaned back in her chair. "No, thanks." Merrick didn't even think twice about it. No way was she going to be under his thumb.

"You're not understanding what I'm offering you. You can quit the firm you're with and be your own boss, have your own clients but every now and again represent someone I need out of jail."

"I hear you loud and clear. The answer is no!" Merrick spit in his face. "Are you feeling me now? Do you understand the words coming out of my mouth?" Merrick hissed.

Her head jerked to the side when he backhanded her. Merrick felt the wig slip. She made a grab for it but it was too late, Joseph Gambino had seen.

"Well, well, well. I think I found your maid." Gambino leaned forward ripping the wig and cap from her head. Her black dreads fell down her back He slapped her across the face again.

All hell broke loose around Merrick when Newton allowed the shield to drop with Stone standing behind her. Before Gambino could react Stone hit him hard across the temple with the butt of a rifle, knocking him unconscious. Merrick shivered. Tears burned behind her eyes. This was it the moment of truth.

Merrick watched Fusion, Newton, and Milla surround her in a protective circle.

"Stone, get Merrick out of here, and you better not let nothing happen to her. I'll take care of Gambino," Milla commanded.

Shots were fired. Merrick could hear shouting and more shots all around her. She caught sight of Pippy as she rolled against the ground and suddenly she was free. She was paralyzed as Merrick watched Pippy hum a knife over Stone's shoulder, which entered a guy's forehead, dropping him instantly.

Merrick nodded to Pippy before Pippy turned away from her. She pulled at Stone's vest bringing him down to her side. "I know you probably hate me right now, but Milla can't be here! You have to get her out of here before it's too late. Nothing else matters, Leave Gambino to me." Fear rose up in Merrick's throat like lava. It was so acute she could taste the bile. "You have to hurry." Merrick pushed him towards Milla.

"Hello, Father."

"No!" Merrick screamed pushing past Stone. She tried to pull Milla away from Gambino, but Milla half turned and quickly grabbed her chin in a vise like grip.

"I have to do this to protect us. I'm tired of living in fear."

"Angelina? My daughter?" Gambino asked.

Before Merrick could warn Milla that Gambino was trying to move. Milla pushed her away without warning, throwing her off balance. Before anyone could react, Milla shoved the assault rifle's mussel against his forehead.

"I'm no daughter of yours. I'm dead to you!" Milla hissed. "You killed my mother! I hate you!"

"I don't understand. I had a funeral. I watched them put you in the ground. How can this be?"

The surprise on his face didn't change how Merrick felt. *He's probably wondering how she pulled it off and not so much as he actually might have missed his own daughter.*

Merrick leaned into Milla and whispered, "Please don't do this. Leave and let me deal with him. Tell him you're lying about being his daughter. He will never stop hunting you, me, the people we love."

"No! Not this time." Milla pushed Merrick away angrily. "This has to end."

Merrick watched how Milla pushed the gun against her father's head. "You can't be the one to kill your own father."

Gambino swiftly moved without warning. Before Merrick could react she stared as two ninja stars punctured his chest. He screamed, falling backwards. Merrick looked over her shoulder. Pippy was standing there.

Pippy winked at her. "Grab her and let's get out of here." Motioning to Merrick.

Shots were fired all around. Merrick watched Pippy's expression change to shock as her hand went to her chest. Blood spread. Pippy had been shot. She started to fall, but Merrick ran forward and pulled her against her. Both of them awkwardly tumbled to the floor. Merrick turned making sure she hit the floor instead of Pippy. They landed hard but she ignored the pain and quickly scrambled from under, her laying her gently down. "How bad is it?" Her hands were shaking as she ran them over the wound.

Pippy gathered Merrick against her chest as she quickly threw a knife that hit dead center in the throat of one of Gambino's men. The gun he held shot off rounds in all directions as he fell.

Merrick was aware when Stone knelt next to her, but the next thing she knew she was shoved down over Pippy's prone body on the floor and Stone shot two of Gambino's men rushing toward them.

"Are you hit?"

His hands searched her body, quickly assessing for damage. She couldn't respond because her body was responding to his touch. A moan slipped past her lips and his hand went to her face moving right and then left.

"Tell me where you are hurt."

All she could do was shake her head to show she wasn't injured. His touch was tender. Maybe there was still a chance he'd listen. She decided she was going to bare her soul and tell him everything when they could get out of here.

Pippy coughed and Merrick's attention was again focused on her. Blood was quickly spreading across her chest.

"We have to stop the blood." Merrick ran to the kitchen drawer and pulled out all of her kitchen towels and ran back. "We can use these." She slid next to Stone.

"Apply pressure to the wound to stop the flow of blood until we can get some help in here."

The blood soaked through the first towel quickly.

"Protect yourself. I'm going to go clean house so we can get her to the hospital."

The gun felt cold against her leg as it slid across the floor. A Fear swamped Merrick. There were so many after them. They were probably outmanned and outgunned.

"Milla, are you good?" Stone asked.

"Yeah. I have this."

"The death of your mother was an accident. I miss her everyday. It was after I lost and buried you something in me died. You were my heart. My flower child, Don't you remember..."

"Stop talking! You son of a bitch. You forget I was there. I watched you kill her with my own eyes. Before that you beat her like a dog. You call that love?" Milla fumed.

"I lost my head when she told me she wanted a divorce. I regret how I treated her. If I had been a better husband and father, I would still have my wife and daughter. Maybe you, Carlos and I can be a family now? You would like that wouldn't you?"

"Don't listen to him, Milla. He's a great story-teller. It's how he makes all his money. He makes people believe his lies, or if they don't, he sends his musclemen to force them into compliance," Merrick stated furious at Gambino for lying to his own daughter.

Merrick cradled Pippy against her on the floor. She added pressure with the towels to stop the flow of blood. She couldn't stop the bleeding. Tears started to burn behind her eyes. Everything was unraveling and it was a huge overload. "I'm so sorry. All of this is my fault."

"I'm going to be okay. It just hurts like hell. It's not the first time I've been shot," Pippy explained.

Merrick jumped and whipped around at the sound of a rifle going off behind her. Gambino screamed. Milla had shot him.

"Does that hurt, daddy dearest?" she asked.

Merrick watched Milla stick the hot barrel of her gun against the wound in his shoulder.

The scream bellowed through the house.

"The apple doesn't fall far from the tree, does it, Father?" Milla mocked him.

"What the hell?"

Merrick watched Sal run to Milla. "What are you doing?" He asked with concern in his voice.

"It's okay, Dad." Milla looked at him.

"What the fuck did you just call him?" Gambino hissed furiously from the floor.

Merrick couldn't believe this was happening. Gambino tried to get up, but Milla shot him again this time in his stomach.

Gambino screamed once again. "You bitch! You're just like your mother."

"You're not so big and powerful without your morons standing in front of you for protection."

"Stop!" Gambino screamed.

"I'd stop talking if I were you." Milla tossed the words at him. "You might just bleed out right here on the floor."

"Are you the person responsible for taking my daughter away from me?" Gambino hissed.

Merrick couldn't take anymore she got up and gently leaned Pippy against the wall. She went to Milla and pushed her against Sal. She could hear things breaking from the fighting and people shooting. "I wouldn't worry so much about who took your daughter away. I'd be more concerned whether you're going to get out of here alive," Merrick hissed.

"It was you. I know it was because you have connections. I'm going to kill you like I did your father, except I'm going to take my time and make you suffer so much more. You took away my family," Gambino threatened.

"Funny thing is, you asshole, you killed your own family when you killed your wife in front of your daughter, but I guess in you're delusional mind it's everybody else's fault. To me you had this coming for a long time," Merrick hissed.

"Sal, take Milla and leave. I'll handle Gambino." Merrick waited for Milla to give in.

"Merrick, you can't let him live. You know this, right?" Milla demanded.

Merrick shook her head in agreement. It was the only way to get her to leave.

Once Sal pulled her from the room. Merrick watched Pippy sag against the wall. In fear she ran to her new friend, forgetting Gambino for a moment to lean down to check her pulse. She was still alive. Thank goodness.

When Merrick stood and turned, Gambino had somehow made it to the forgotten gun on the floor and was pointing it at her. She watched him pull the trigger. She even felt when the bullet entered her body, but it didn't fell, more like a slow motion film being played out. Merrick was falling slowly to the ground. It was going to hurt because she couldn't get her arms to work so she could break her fall. From behind her, she felt hands grab her and slowly put her on the ground.

Her eyes closed. They were just to heavy to try to open them again, but she could hear things around her. She was so cold. she wished someone would get the blanket from the closet. A gun went off close by. Voices were a buzz. Her last thoughts were of Stone. She hoped he was safe. The darkness pulled her under into the empty void.

***

The steady beep of her alarm clock dragged her slowly out of a semi-conscious slumber. Her first thought was she'd have to buy a new clock soon because this one must be broken. It didn't sound normal. Her eyelids were heavy and she fought to stay asleep, but now the sound of voices added to the annoying noises. The voices were very angry. *Did I leave the television on?* When her eyelids fluttered open, it was too bright and she hurriedly shut them. Disoriented, she tried to turn on her side away from the light. She screamed at the sudden pain ripping through her body. Merrick opened her eyes to see a nurse standing over her, holding her down.

Now she was really confused. *Why is a nurse in my house? Where are Newton and Fusion? They know not to allow a stranger into our home.*

"You can't turn over right now. You'll rip your stitches and start to bleed again."

At that moment Merrick moved, and the pain made her catch her breath. That's when the memories surfaced, reminding her of what had happened. Vaguely, she remembered the ambulance ride. Glimpses of nurses sticking needles in her. They wouldn't allow her to sleep. She looked around and realized she was in the hospital emergency room with the door opened. Sal stood outside talking on the phone.

"What do you mean, he's escaped?"

Merrick made eye contact with Sal as he turned. He shut the phone with a snap and rushed toward her. He looked old. Wrinkles lined his face and arms. When did that happen? Sal looked worried but his eyes were so full of love.

"Who escaped?" Merrick wanted to know. She tried to sit up, but the damn nurse wouldn't let her.

"Don't you worry about that. Right now all I want from you missy is to get well. How are you feeling?"

Merrick felt his hand tremble as he touched her face.

"We almost lost you, Merrick. The bullet lodged in your collar bone close to your heart."

"I'm okay, Pops. Don't you worry." The nurse made noise under her breath which made Merrick angry. When she got her attention, Merrick gave her the courtroom evil eye. "Do you mind leaving us alone?" It wasn't a question, and the nurse must have heard it in the tone Merrick used. The nurse huffed and puffed as she left, leaving them alone.

Merrick dismissed her instantly to turn her attention to Sal. "Is Milla alright?

Pippy? Oh my goodness, where is Stone? Newton and Fusion?

"Help me up. I need to get out of here." She tried to get up but Sal forced her back down against the pillows.

"No way, missy! They are both fine and Stone is fine. Fusion and Newton are here in your room. I couldn't get them to stay home. Newton is doing his magic. You would think they're your children."

"They are my children, Pops." She smiled for the first time but only fleeting. "Gambino? That's who you are talking about, isn't it? He's still alive?

"Oh my god. He is. You can't lie to me. I see it all over your face."

"Yes, he's alive. He escaped after they brought him from surgery. His men came, dressed like nurses I presume and grabbed him.

"Tell me what happened because I don't remember much. I can't believe Milla didn't finish him off.

"We can talk about this later, after you've rested. It was a close call, young lady. Your mother and aunt have been worried sick. So, do me a favor and just catch up on some sleep."

"No one is safe. You know that, don't you? I have to get out of here, Pops!" Desperation consumed her. "He'll go after Milla and the family. Not to mention Stone and Pippa." Painfully she forced herself to sit up and fisted her hand in his shirt. "You." Merrick panted. "He's going to come full force after you. I can't lose you to him like I did my father. I just can't. You need bodyguards." She hissed the words out through gritted teeth.

"He's going to be out for blood and there will be no stopping him now. Gambino will want us all dead."

"I have everyone on lockdown. Don't you worry."

"You're not listening to me." Frustrated, Merrick weakly resisted. The pain ripped through her at the slightest of moments, giving Sal the advantage as he gently but firmly put her back against the pillows. "You, young lady, I need you well, so you're going to stay here until the doctor tells you differently. I'm about to make you angry, but I know you love me so you'll forgive me. Nurse?"

Merrick watched the same nurse who had stomped out come back in looking all snarky; totally ignoring the evil looks Merrick was sending her. She looked at Sal inquiringly.

"May I help you?"

She even batted her eyelashes at him. That woman was flirting with him openly in front of her.

"I think Merrick should be sleeping, don't you?"

"Don't do this, Pops! Let me help. You need me." Merrick persisted, turning to the nurse and giving her a dirty look.

"Why, of course, lots of rest is what the doctor ordered."

"Why, you dirty dog," Merrick fumed, watching Nurse Hatchet run from the room looking a little bit too pleased with herself. "I don't have time to sleep, Pops. I need to get out of here. It's not safe! You're not safe!"

"Don't worry about you or me. I have things covered. I just want you to rest and get well, not to mention both Newton and Fusion are here for backup."

The nurse came back quickly, bursting through the door carrying a syringe. If she didn't know any better, Merrick was almost certain that Nurse Hatchet as she called her was skipping in glee as she went to an IV and inserted the needle.

It was the way the nurse thumped the line, making sure all was okay. Part of her knew she was only doing her job, but Merrick couldn't stop the rage coiling in her belly. She felt so damned helpless. Merrick turned to Sal.

"Please. Don't make me stay. I need to be doing something, like protecting all of you. It's what I do." Her words began to slur. Damn, she could already feel the effects of whatever Nurse Hatchet had added to her IV. Against her will, her eyelids started to droop. "This is so not fair." She didn't know if she actually said it out loud or it was a mere thought as the darkness dragged her under.

★ ★ ★

"There must be a mistake in her chart."

"What do you mean?" Sal asked.

"This can't be Defense Attorney Hardin. She doesn't look anything like her." The nurse peered down to get a closer inspection. "If that's not her, I should call the cops, but I hate her. She's on the take. That bitch is a sellout to our city."

"No, Merrick is not a sellout, so watch your mouth before I report you. In fact I should call in your superior and have a chat with her about your conduct. This is Merrick, but this is private information so please keep this information to yourself. It's a life and death situation, and no one else can find out." Sal grabbed the nurse's arm waiting for her to answer.

"I won't say anything for now, but I'm not making any promises." The nurse yanked her arm from Sal's grip and stomped out.

Sal waited until the nurse closed the door before he turned to where Newton and Fusion were hiding. "Keep watch and listen for anything suspicious. Newton, you call me immediately if you need me. I'll be wearing the ear piece you gave me. I have someone at the door, but sometimes that doesn't mean much." Sal left, closing the door.

Newton recognized the nurse from earlier as she pushed the door open. When she entered another person came in behind her. She pushed the tall orderly toward the bed.

"Is this her?" the nurse whispered.

"Yes. Go stand guard outside the room and don't allow anyone inside, or you won't get paid when I tell Gambino you didn't hold up your end of the deal."

"Be quick about it. The nurses change shifts in about thirty minutes."

The nurse left, shutting the door behind her.

The orderly pulled out his cell phone and made a call. "It's a go. I'm at the window." He pulled back the curtains and waited. Within minutes a loud thump hit the glass from outside. The orderly on the inside pulled out two round disks with handles from the inside of his orderly coat and suctioned them to the glass. He pulled on them make sure they were snug.

The orderly waited impatiently, cursing toward the window to whoever was out there. At some point there was a muffled pounding against the glass until the nurse grabbed the big suction cups and pulled. A loud popping noise interrupted the quietness. The wind blew through the curtains from the height of room.

"Help me get through the window, you moron."

"If you call me that one more time, you're going to need hospital care." The orderly reached out and grabbed a foot and pulled someone into the room.

"Is the nurse keeping watch?"

"If she wasn't, with all the noise you were making, we would be in handcuffs for sure by now."

The man in a harness walked to the bed. "She's a little bitty thing. She shouldn't be too hard to get through the window. What bothers me is why not just kill her and be done with this shit."

"The boss said, don't hurt one hair on her head. So, let's get her through the window and get out of here before the shift change. I just got out of the joint, and I don't want to go back in."

The other man went to the foot of the bed. "How do you want to do this?

From behind Newton removed the hologram hiding himself and Fusion. Fusion growled deeply in her throat, stalking them.

"Gentlemen. I would advise you not to touch my charge, or I'll have to take control of the situation."

The men laughed.

Fusion jumped on the end of the bed, baring her nail teeth.

"Don't attack them, Fusion. It could draw unwanted attention. Instead store their profiles for another time."

One of the men shoved Fusion from the rear, trying to dislodge the cat from the bed. Fusion hissed and turned quickly before the man could move. With nails extended, she swiped with one of her black polished metal paws and ripped the front of the orderly's coat to shreds.

"Holy shit, that cat almost gutted me!"

"Fusion! Stand down!" Newton commanded.

The orderly slapped his neck and fell to the floor, unconscious. The man in the harness went limp, and the cord pulled his unconscious body all the way back to the window with his body slumped over.

"Fusion, gather the darts from their necks."

Newton shot Merrick in the neck with a neutralizing dart. He needed her awake immediately. It was imperative that he get Merrick to safety. Men were on the floor, the window was cut open, all hell was about to break loose, and he needed Merrick nowhere around when it did.

The knob on the door began to turn. The nurse from earlier peered inside but seeing the orderly at the window apparently waiting for the other person. She closed the door.

"That was a close call, Fusion."

Merrick stirred but didn't awaken.

"Time to wake up, Merrick." Newton chimed. He sounded the alarm he used for when it was time for her to get up for work. Within minutes Merrick's eyes fluttered opened. "It worked."

"Merrick, are you with us?" Newton asked.

Fusion jumped on the bed to lay over her.

"God, you're heavy." Merrick's hand shook as she touched the Jaguar.

"Where am I?"

"In a hospital, but we need to get you out of here. I sedated the two men on the floor. I think they might be Gambino's goons. I'm not sure who's on the roof but we shouldn't be here when he figures out that something is wrong."

"Ok, let me get my clothes on. Fusion, I need my extra clothes." It took longer than she wanted to get dressed in the black cargo pants and black shirt along with black slip-on sneakers. Her arms and legs didn't want to co-operate. She was weak and in a lot of pain.

Movement on the floor made her stop getting dressed. She grabbed the nearest thing, a chair. Merrick swung it at the man moving on the floor three or four times until the man didn't move.

Sweat beaded on her brow, legs wobbly she sat down hard in a chair.

"I just need a minute, Newton. I'm beat."

Newton moved next to the chair. "Sit on me so I can get us out of here."

"I can do that." Merrick huffed and puffed until she was finally on him.

"I'm going to take a nap."

Chapter 11

Sirens blared closer and closer, putting Merrick on alert. She pushed herself up into a sitting position, looking around. They had only made it to the ground floor at the main lobby. She realized suddenly she had fallen asleep due to the drugs in her system.

By the time she made it to the door to leave, the whole front of the hospital was surrounded with police. Lights were flashing, and a team of men ran right past her toward the entrance.

Unseen, the three of them moved through the crowd. People were coming out of the woodwork to see what was going on, making it easier to get lost among the crowd.

"Take me to my father's grave." Merrick waited until they were well away from the growing crowd of people before she gave Newton direction.

"Do you think that is safe, my lady?"

"I don't care if it's safe. I almost lost my life. I need this, Newton. Please understand."

"Yes, my lady. We're on our way. Should I inform your father of your plans?"

"No. Wait, did you tell him about what happened in the hospital?" Merrick needed to know so she could carefully consider her options.

"Yes, of course. He dictated to me to keep him abreast of all issues.

"In that case you can tell him I'm safe and I need a few minutes to collect my thoughts, but I'm coming home. I'm tired of running. This has to end." It was time, she thought. The responsibility and worries weighed heavily upon her shoulders. Her body hurt like a freight train had hit her. Sometimes she didn't know which end was up with all the lies she had told. The double life was a necessity, but at some point she just wanted a break. Fighting injustice was not an easy task on a daily basis with everyone wanting her to represent them.

It was what she did on the down low, the part she hid from the citizens. If they only knew what she had done to protect and keep New Orleans safe. Granted, it never seemed to end. As soon as Merrick stopped one criminal, a new one took its place.

Seeing her mother after all this time had triggered these thoughts. After seeing her mom and realizing how much she missed her and needed her in her life hit her like a ton of bricks. She wished her father were alive. Right now she could sure use his help.

"Yes, my lady."

The interruption was appreciated. She was having a temporary break down. Usually she never lived in the what if's.

Newton turned to Fusion. "Be on guard."

Getting to the cemetery didn't take long. Only a few people were roaming the grounds, visiting the dead. They rode slowly past many tombs before they stopped in front of the mausoleum where her father was buried. It took a few moments for Merrick to collect herself before she tried to get off the motorcycle. She took a deep breath and forced her body to comply. Her body didn't react well, causing her to clumsily fall to her knees when her legs gave out. Fusion came up next to her and leaned against Merrick until she pushed her head under her hand.

"Fusion wants you to use her to stand when your ready," Newton commented.

"I'm fine, you two, just a little weak." Once she finally stood up with the assistance of Fusion, she half turned to Newton. "I need the key."

A small compartment on the motorcycle opened. Even if Newton were to catch fire, God forbid, the hidden compartment was fireproof. Anything inside would be safe. It was also burglar safe. "Stand guard, you two. I'm going in alone."

It took a minute to open the door. Not only was there a locked door, there was also a combination keypad installed. She never understood that part, but it had been there as long as she could remember. Even when her grandparents passed away, it was there. Then it was an older version but it had been replaced with a newer style.

It was dark inside with shadows casting off the walls. Along the sides were a few old coffins. Once she stepped inside a light came on automatically, probably with a pressure plate under the flooring. Against each coffin held a name plate displaying a family picture. A small Victorian antique seatee was positioned in a good spot in case anyone needed to sit. The place was kept cleaned probably by the groundskeeper.

"I really did it this time, Poppy and Grandfather." Her fingers lingered on her grandfather's picture. "I have let the family down and endangered our family." Tears burned down her cheeks.

"Poppy," she went to her father against the other wall. He was at the top shelf. "I almost had Gambino. I crippled his cartel, but he's on to me now. He sent his men to kill me, but I escaped. Now I have no choice but to kill him so I can keep our family safe."

She started to cry in earnest. I can't lose Mom. I just can't, or Sal or Maria. They're all I have."

In her despair, Merrick leaned her forehead upon the coffin. Absently her fingers traced the details over the outside. In the quietness of the mausoleum, the loud click made her startle in surprise.

A drawer that ran the length of her father's coffin slid open. A gasp of surprise escaped Merrick when she found it was filled with weapons. Now she understood all the security measures that had been put into place.

She ran her fingers over the outside of the drawer to see if it could be lifted. When it did indeed lift, she found a bullet proof vest inside along with some different maps and handwritten notes about locations and more.

Without delay she ran outside to Newton and raised the seat. Long ago she had stored a duffle bag inside the storage area. Merrick wasn't even sure if it was still there, but she needed something to carry the weapons. To her surprise it was still there to her surprise and quickly grabbed it and raced back inside. Time was of the essence.

As she packed the guns inside the duffle bag, she made sure each weapon was loaded and fully functional. The duffle bag didn't take long to fill, and she must have triggered something in the drawer because another coffin along the opposite wall opened.

Inside the coffin's lid was a flat screen television. It was custom made from one end to the other. It was narrow in height, but made up for it in width. After a few moments, it powered on automatically and Merrick was staring at her father's and grandfather's faces.

Their voices sounded so real. Her father and grandfather looked so handsome and alive. It made it so hard to realize they weren't actually there.

Her grandfather and her dad gathered all the intel she would need and packed everything in his coffin. There were detailed maps of Gambino's different hideouts, plus blueprints of the Sugar Cane Company he owned and operated while he pushed out his drugs. They had provided all the details on how to cripple Gambino's cartel for good. They put everything together toward the end as a fail-safe method in case they failed to crush Gambinio's empire.

Her father's voice came across. Merrick couldn't stop the tears as she stood in front of the television. Her fingers reached out and traced his face over the screen. She bowed her head for a moment, caught up in emotions she couldn't seem to control.

"As a result of you finding this, an alarm has alerted certain people who will be your support. Even though we have perished, we do have friends and family, fighting for our cause. Take care of mother and Milla, Sal and Maria. Tell them they are loved."

"Yes. Yes, Father, I will." When she heard her own voice, she captured her mouth with her hand to stop the flow of words. She pushed herself away from the television, feeling the resolve fill her. Her spine straightened. She stood proud.

"Merrick."

At the door she heard her name and turned to the television. It was her father's voice once again. "I love you princess, You'll always be my sunshine. Until we meet again." The television went blank and the coffin closed as if that never happened.

Her father had loved her and had protected her even through death. A choked sob escaped as she opened the door. Merrick screamed and fell into the arms of Stone. His strong hands settled her when she faltered, firm but gentle as he pulled her into the protection of his body. She struggled against him until her brain caught up with who held her.

"Stone?" she questioned. Her voice trembled.

"Yes."

She watched him lean down so close she could smell him. His breath raced over her skin, sending goose bumps up and down her arms. She shivered.

"Later, when we're alone, I'm going to spank that beautiful ass."

She giggled, closing her eyes while she collected herself.

"You're not alone any longer. You understand? Where you go, I go."

Merrick heard the anger, the hurt in his words. She searched his face and read the truth in his eyes.

Movement behind Stone caught her attention, and there stood Sal and Milla, shoulder to shoulder, armed to the gills. There were others she figured who were part of

Milla's and Sal's team. People she never knew and some she did recognize stood there, all holding weapons.

"I don't understand?" Merrick looked around.

A woman with grey hair appearing maybe in her fifties but looking like a mean-ass grandma stepped forth. There was no fat on her, and she was sporting a gun which weighed at least seventy pounds.

"Your father and grandfather helped all of us at one time or another and sometimes more than once. We formed a secret service if you want to call us that. We pulled together to fight and keep our citizens protected. All of us have been watching over you, secretly protecting your identity from the mafia and crime-lords because that is what your father and grandfather would have done, and we have people watching your mother. She's never been alone."

"I don't know what to say. I'm so humbled. Thank you."

Through the tears rolling down her face, she watched silently as Sal and Milla walked up to her, "Did you know about this?"

Merrick watched Sal shrug his shoulders. "Yes. You can say that I'm the one in charge."

"Milla?"

"Only recently. After my last tour, I went to see Mom. I was lured in, and we all discussed self-defense for Mom. She had no clue. I told her we needed to join a gym and get into shape. At first she argued I was already in shape, but I told her I needed to keep it that way. In the end she's lost weight and is more fit and limber. Secretly Milla and her dad talked to the owners of the gym into giving a class for self-defense. I told her we needed to take the class in case we ever get mugged."

"I see. Why didn't you include me?" Merrick asked, feeling a little hurt.

"Because you wouldn't have allowed it," Sal put in. "You would have interfered. I didn't want you worrying about something that was out of your hands. Plus, you have enough on your plate."

"Are you trying to say I'm pigheaded?" Merrick raised a eyebrow.

"Well aren't you?" Milla teased.

Without answering, she changed the subject. "Everyone come inside. I have something to show you," Merrick said as she pulled Stone through the doors. She went to the coffin and ran her fingers inside of it, unsure of where she touched before, but finally the other casket opened and the television automatically turned on.

The crowd of people gasped in surprise but seemed to relax when they saw the television.

Merrick pushed Sal and Milla to the front as the TV started. Merrick watched her sister's and Sal's face's as the recording started to replay. She heard Milla's indrawn breath. Several people made loud, shocked noises. From behind her a woman wept. When the recording was over, the casket closed just like before. No one moved.

Sal coughed and went to her grandfather's opened coffin where all the maps and information was stored. Merrick opened the duffle bag.

"Be careful. All the weapons are loaded and ready," she warned.

While they went over the plans and the maps, Merrick walked outside to Newton. Stone followed, searching the area making sure it was safe. She smiled secretly.

"Send out two drones and recon his house. Send one on the factory. Let's make sure of Gambino's location before we send anyone out. Keep me updated of what's happening out there," Merrick ordered.

"I'm on it. Would you like one to go the shack? Just to be on the safe side?" Newton inquired.

"Yes, that is a great idea. Thank you," Merrick said. "You are the best."

"I have to agree on that score, but add Fusion as well," Stone commented.

They walked back in as Sal was dividing people into two teams. "I sent drones out to the house, the factory, and the shack to watch them. We need to find out which location Gambino might be in. That way we're not going in blind" Merrick announced.

"That's a good idea," Milla said.

"You're coming with us, Milla," Stone interrupted. "I'm not taking any excuses."

Merrick watched him take off running to the entrance when shouting started outside. Two black armored hummers had pulled up. As the men started to exit the vehicles, they were greeted at gunpoint.

"Stand down!" Stone barked.

The sound echoed off the walls of the mausoleum. There was a pause among the crowd.

"These are my men who will be spilt up among each team. They are skilled and at your service. They have been informed of the details of what's going on," Stone commanded out loud.

"I never seen you on the phone," Merrick stated, curious.

"You weren't always with me. I thought extra help could be useful for a successful mission." Stone continued with calm.

Fusion brushed up against her leg, using body language for her to follow. Some of these people didn't know her, only her father and Sal.

"I'll be back," she told Stone over her shoulder, already working her way through the crowd towards Newton. She pulled out a Bluetooth earpiece and inserted it in her ear.

"Mistress, the drone over the residence of Anthony Gambino is showing no activity. The factory has people there, but again there is no evidence of any of his men or him.

"The drone hasn't made it to the shack. It's updating now with the new coordinates I implemented to show the surrounding area of the shack of any approaching vehicles or boats."

A red icon popped on and another and another until four icons steadily moved across Newton's monitor. Newton typed something into the computer and zoomed in, indicating not one but four black suvs flying down the interstate, and three icons more showing movement in the water heading toward the shack.

"Come on," Stone commanded, grabbing Merrick's hand and pulling her toward the mausoleum. "We need to inform Sal so we can plan our strategy of attack."

Merrick broke away from Stone and ran straight into Sal. Her fingers twisted in his shirt nervously. "We have to get Mom and Maria out of the house. Now! Gambino's on his way with a small army."

"Calm down. Calm down, sweetheart. They're not at the shack."

"Where are they?" Merrick felt the knots in her gut tighten more.

"Do you think I would leave them unprotected? They're not at the shack; they're at home with the dogs."

"The dogs? That's it?" Merrick tried to bolt, but Sal stopped her.

"No, not just the dogs. I have a couple of my men guarding them.

"That's not enough. Let's hurry so we can get moving." Merrick almost yelled.

"I've never seen you act like this, Merrick. Normally you have a cool head about you," Sal observed.

"It's my mom and Maria. If anything happens to them... It'll be my fault." Merrick started to pace. "Look, you go ahead and tell the men what you want and send them where they need to be. I'm going to head out now so I can get there. I can't wait. Call me through Newton."

Merrick ran out and jumped on Newton. "Fusion, get to shack and take out anyone who stands in your way, and send back intel. If they try to get to Mom or Maria, kill them."

Merrick hurriedly put on a helmet, but she still heard Stone scream her name as Newton quickly pulled off. She wasn't going to stop. No way would she give Gambino a chance at her mother. He would love to kill her, especially now that he knew his daughter was alive.

Another thing, all hell will break loose if and when he finds out I've been protecting the eyewitness. Personally, I do believe he'd risk a small fortune on my head.

If Gambino gets to mom before I can get there, everything I've done will be for nothing because he'll kill her. He might wait until I get there, but for him that will be his finest hour. That's how he works. Fear. Merrick hated to admit it but that was what was riding her at this point, pure one hundred percent fear.

"Mistress, they have arrived at the entrance of the neighborhood. I told the front gate personnel to stand down and allow them through."

"That was a good idea. Thank you for thinking on your feet." Merrick laughed nervously at her terrible sense of humor.

"Milla is calling in. She would like to speak to you."

"Connect the Bluetooth so I can answer the phone. Sal is supposed to call as well."

"Go for Merrick," already knowing Milla was going to be angry.

"Are you crazy?" The angry voice hissed through the Bluetooth. "Please tell me now that after all this time you have finally gone off the deep end. I'm coming up hot behind you. We do this together. He's my father, and I'm going to be the one to kill him. I do realize you have your own set of rules, but not this time. You understand me?" Milla fumed.

Merrick couldn't get the words out because she had always protected her sister.

It didn't matter that she wasn't her blood. It was the way Milla came to the family that always left Merrick with a protective nature.

Her father had been undercover watching the Gambino's homestead, and in broad daylight he had heard gunfire. He had called it in, but before he could get to the house, a little girl had come tearing out of the house screaming at the top of her lungs.

Her father had grabbed the little girl as Gambino's goons had chased them down the driveway, firing their guns. Police units had come rushing to the house, surrounding them.

Her father had run with the little girl past the cars to a safe distance. A bullet had hit him, and although he had faltered, but hadn't dropped her. Blood had quickly covered him and the little girl. Gambino had seen his daughter covered in blood and screamed before he shot his own men. Her father had instinctively told the little girl to play dead. She had gone limp in his arms.

Later he had brought Milla to the house and had sent Merrick to bed so he could talk with her mother privately. After a few minutes he had told his wife the story as the child had clung to him. Merrick had heard every word since she hadn't gone to bed but had hidden close enough to hear. Since then she had sworn that no one would ever hurt Milla again.

"Merrick, are you listening to me?"

"Yes, I am," Merrick said as she watched the motorcycle pull up next to hers. It was sleek, red and fast.

"I know," Milla's voice came through the Bluetooth.

Merrick shook her head. "You know what?" she asked stalling for time because she had a feeling she wasn't going to like what Milla had to say.

"I know your trying to protect me. Again. I love you for that I do, I swear, but you know in your heart I need to do this."

"I don't want you to carry the burden of this for the rest of your life. You should allow me to do this," Merrick coached.

"Sis, you have been protecting all of us for years. Living a double life, hiding who you are from everyone. You have lived the lie for so long sometimes I think you don't even know who you are anymore, the real you. Damn it, look at me."

Merrick reluctantly glanced over.

"Do you? Do you know who you are? You know, my sister who used to laugh and tickle me until I about peed my pants?" Milla questioned.

"Barely," the hoarse whisper came out against Merrick's will, but she couldn't lie to her. Not her. They were close, as close as she could be with anyone.

"You have to let me go. I have to do this for you, for me, but most of all I have to do this for my mother. Her face haunts me to this day. Every time I close my eyes, I relive my mother's eyes empty of life. She died trying to protect me. She wanted a good life for us, but he wouldn't allow us to leave. I was the cause of her death. Now is the time I to set us all free. I'm not saying you have to walk away. You can have my back, but Gambino is mine."

Merrick tried to wipe the tears from her eyes, but the helmet made it difficult. "Okay, you win, but just stay close in case you need me."

A black double-cab pickup pulled up behind them and blew the horn. It was Sal and Stone. Newton swerved to the side and slowed down until he was by the driver's side of the truck. Milla did the same on the passenger side. Men were in the back seat dressed in black and putting black eye grease under their eyes to deflect glare.

Merrick smiled at Stone. She couldn't help the ear-to-ear grin. He was there, solid and real, and he was there for her. He was so yummy and gorgeous and hers. He smiled, and her heart wanted to jump out of her chest. She didn't understand it, and she really didn't care how it had happened, but she was happy it did. Now she understood her parents' love. It scared the shit out of her. Could this love be like her parents? Could it survive through the years? Could he love her as much as she loved him? Questions, so many questions. The lawyer in her wanted to dissect it, but she knew better than that.

"Hey, beautiful, you forgot something, didn't you?"

The voice that came through the Bluetooth was Stone's. It sent sparks of awareness down her spine.

"What did I forget?" she asked innocently.

"Me!"

"No, sexy, I didn't. It was a test to see if you would follow me into hell," Merrick tossed the words at him. Another test to see how he was going answer.

"I'll always pass any test you throw at me. Do you know why?" he challenged.

"I might, but I'd rather if you explained it to me in detail.

"That can be arranged. Later though, when we're done with all this, say tonight?"

"It's a date! So, don't get yourself shot up or anything," Merrick teased.

"You either! And that's an order you better listen to."

"I don't mean to interrupt your conversation, but the SUVS have arrived and the ducks in the water are approaching the dock.

"Fuck! Fuck! Fuck!" She swore vehemently. "Those assholes are going to tear up my favorite house. This has always been my safe place. If they do, they're going to pay," Merrick swore again.

"Please be safe, Mom, Maria," she mumbled to herself. Fear slithered up her spine. Her stomach was in knots.

"We need to hurry!" Merrick screamed into the ear piece.

"Don't panic! Listen to me. We're going to get to them. You can't just go blazing in there without using your head," Sal commanded.

"I have your back, Merrick. We will get your mother and Maria out safe. I swear, if one hair on their heads is harmed, they will pay with their lives," Stone promised.

They pulled into the neighborhood quietly and unseen, as Newton covered them within a soundproof protective shield. They moved down the street side by side, quiet, invisible, scanning the area for snipers or any of Gambino's muscle waiting to ambush them.

An explosion rocked the ground. Newton lost traction and so did Milla, but they fought to keep their balance. A truck ahead of them swerved off the road when part of a tin roof landed in front of it.

Ahead raging flames leaped towards the heavens with a veil of black smoke billowing across the horizon. Another explosion rocked the earth, sending more black smoke into the air. Flaming debris landed in the water and streets. The sound of some of the neighbors screaming in panic reached Merrick. Smoke filled the road like a heavy fog, making their approach dangerous. At least if there were snipers out, they couldn't see them coming.

Merrick stopped Newton in the middle of the street, choking back on a sob. "Momma! Maria!" Merrick screamed, jumping off of Newton, staring in the direction of the explosions.

Sal signaled the different teams to head out. Sal's hand gripped her wrist. "Go with Stone, and be careful. She felt him kiss her forehead, gathering Milla to them.

"Remember I love the two of you. Milla, you are Maria's and my daughter, our family. We love you more than you'll ever know."

Merrick hugged them tight. "Stay alive. I need you."

Milla squeezed her and whispered. "I love you, Dad, Merrick. I have to do this. After this, we're free from living in the shadows."

"I'm sorry to interrupt, but there's a team moving away from the house toward the north and one moving to the south. Some of dock and the back porch, are on fire." Newton informed.

"Go, Fusion! Guard Mom and Maria!" Merrick screamed the command.

Fusion growled a warning, baring her sharp nail teeth, and took off at a dead run, turning invisible as she flew across the ground.

"It's time to spilt up," Sal announced. "The house is about two klicks."

Merrick stood on shaky legs as she watched Sal and some of Stone's men walk into the woods surrounding the area. Fear left a nasty taste in her mouth. Her stomach knotted tight enough to make her want to throw up.

"I sent the best of my team with Sal. I left nothing to chance. If something goes down, your father will be protected even at the cost of their lives."

Confidence rolled off of him, giving her the added strength she was missing to push ahead. "I just want this to be over so we can go home."

"Let's get this done." Stone rallied off with Milla, pulling Merrick under his arm. "We stick together at all times. If there is trouble we stand back to back and take it on. Understood?"

"Yes, Daddy! Damn it if Stone doesn't sound just like Dad. Urgh, can you try not to?" Milla complained.

Merrick shook her head and pushed Stone hard. "Enough! We need to get a move on you two."

"I know, Sis. I'm worried about Mom, and this is how I deal with stress," Milla explained.

Stone moved ahead of them, staying in the shadows as much as possible. Birds chirped. Dogs barked, but otherwise the neighborhood was eerily quiet. There wasn't a neighbor out cutting grass or tending their gardens. The old man who sat out everyday on his pier to fish was nowhere to be seen.

Fear for her mother and Maria made Merrick extremely afraid. The adrenaline raced through her veins like a freight train. She tried to listen when Stone or Milla spoke, but all she could hear was her own heartbeat ringing in her ears. Merrick tried to read their lips but it was impossible.

Milla stopped them using a hand signal. Merrick leaned against the house, searching for movement. Three boats pulled up against the bank because the pier was on fire. A dozen of men were pouring out racing across the lawn, armed and dangerous.

"Get behind me," Stone stormed.

Before Merrick moved from her vantage point, two men went down, dead, then another. She pulled Milla with her as Stone moved into position. The sound of gun fire popped as the remaining men fired shots as they ran for cover.

The suppressor on Stone's sniper rifle didn't quiet the gun when he fired. Her ears popped finally so she could hear what was going on. When Stone ran across one of the neighbors' yards, hunched low, Merrick followed. Milla fired, taking down a man on the roof of her own house.

Shadows grew as the sun started its descent behind on the horizon. Time seemed to stand still as they slowly moved forward.

"No!" Milla screamed as she fell to the ground a few feet ahead of her.

Merrick threw down her gun and hurried to her side. "What's wrong? Where are you hit?" That's when she saw and heard one of Sal's dogs.

"I tripped over her," Milla cried. "It's Sabrina, she's mine. She's been shot."

"She's still alive though. That's a good sign." Merrick pulled out a bandana from one of her deep pockets. Merrick gently pushed Milla away so she could tie the handkerchief around the wound to stop the bleeding. "We'll come back for her as soon as we can. I need you to focus because I can't leave you here. You'd be a sitting duck."

"What are you doing?" Milla's panicked voice seemed really loud.

Merrick dragged the dog until she could hide her so nobody else would find her. "She'll be safe here until we come for her."

"Thank you."

"You're welcome." Merrick squeezed her. "Let's get this finished."

"Are you two finished?" Without waiting for an answer. "Move your asses. You're both sitting ducks." Stone hissed a warning.

Merrick went back for her rifle on the ground, but it wasn't there. Stone was holding it out.

"Don't put this down again."

Merrick watched Stone shake his head as he pushed it into her hands.

"What? You have something to say?" Merrick asked.

"Not a thing." He jerked the head of his rifle instead.

Merrick ran to where Stone pointed and hid in the shadows. A screamed raised the hairs on the back of her neck as she plastered herself against the side of the shed. Then another. Females. Without looking she knew it was her mother and Maria. She fell to the ground and rolled so she could see through the rifle's scope.

Through the haze of anger she briefly glanced toward Stone and watched him grab Milla before she could run straight into trouble. Merrick put the gun against her shoulder and looked through the scope. Someone

166

laid gunfire, hitting the ground in front of them, spewing dirt. The men who held them dragged both women back into the house.

Chapter 12

Merrick shot one round, dropping the last man before he could enter the house. The glow from the fire burning showed the people right inside the door. Merrick heard a scream just as Merrick caught sight of Fusion attacking someone from the inside. The person standing too close to the door fell to his death, landing in the doorway, shot dead. Someone else dropped down to move him so the door would shut. One of their own took him out as his body dropped on top of the other.

Flames from the workshop gave off an eerie glow, but also gave off enough light to see the area. Gambino's men were crawling everywhere. Out the corner of her eye, she caught movement heading toward the house. Stone's men were wearing identifying armbands. One of the men saluted Stone as they passed close by. They were rushing the house, taking deadly shots and dropping Gambino's men one at a time.

Without waiting, Merrick moved away from the wall she'd used for cover, aimed and took the shot, taking out one of Gambino's men. A bullet whizzed by her ear making her flinch, but she kept pace with the other team.

Stone and Milla moved on each side of her, doing their own damage. Dead bodies were scattered everywhere. The body count would be high, but they had signed their own death warrant by taking her mom and Maria.

Stone went down hard, landing on one knee. "Son of a bitch!" He grabbed his left shoulder.

Merrick pushed him gently against the side of a parked truck belonging to one of her neighbors. Milla was right next to her, squatting low to keep them safe while Merrick hovered over Stone.

"How bad is it?" Merrick's voice trembled when she could get her voice to work.

"I'm okay. It's just a flesh wound."

Merrick didn't realize she had grabbed her chest in fear until Stone took her hand into his.

"I'm okay. Remember I was shot a lot worse recently."

"Yes, but now you're mine, and I can't imagine being without you."

Stone kissed her hard on the lips.

"That's not going to happen." He stood. "Let's go get our mom and Maria.

They ended up behind the other team behind the house. Sal was there. "I have to get inside. Those assholes have my wife and her mom."

"I know. They all die today," Stone said.

Sal handed two smoke grenades to Stone. "Go around to the side of the house and throw these in towards the front of the house."

"No problem," Stone said.

Before he could move, Sal commanded, "Whistle after you get them in."

"I'll be back." Stone kissed Merrick so fast she didn't have time to respond before he was gone.

Within a few seconds Milla heard a faint whistle. "Dad, it's done," Milla said. "Let's go get Mom." She took the other two smoke grenades from him and threw them through the hole in the door window.

"Put these on," Sal instructed as he tossed them gas masks from his backpack. While they geared up, a huge man standing on the other side of Sal kicked in the back door. He barreled in first like a freight train.

Merrick's heart was racing as she put her arm through the strap and shouldered the rifle just as Stone returned. Instead she pulled out a Glock 19 handgun and entered after Stone. Milla was behind her like a second skin.

"Stay close Sis."

Merrick nodded shock her head in agreement, letting Milla know she heard her sister's muffled voice. She reached back and searched for her hand and felt it when Milla gripped it tight and squeezed. She quickly turned and glanced at her sister. They smiled at each other, and Merrick nodded in agreement.

Gunfire had already started on the other side of the house. Merrick heard raised voices and suddenly someone screamed. The hairs on the back of Merrick's neck stood on end. A man yelled. Merrick recognized the voice; it was Gambino.

When Merrick tried to pass Stone, he gripped her arms and held her tightly, making her realize he wasn't pleased that she wanted to bolt into the house without him. He shook his head in denial and pointed to her and Milla to stay with him.

All Merrick could do was agree by nodding her head and allowing her shoulders to slump in acknowledgment. He gripped her free hand and brought it to his chest, holding it against his heart. She looked up at him, and she could barely see him wink.

Off to the right side two men were fighting fiercely. Both Merrick and Milla instantly realized one of the men was Sal. Before Merrick could react Milla dropped and rolled and came up behind the fight with two long knives in her hands. Without hesitation she shoved the knives into the other person's body all the way to the hilt. The man dropped, dead.

As Milla bent down to pull the knives out, a man rushed at her from behind. Merrick watched Stone run and hit him dead in the chest with his feet, knocking him off balance. Stone rolled and came up behind Milla. Before the man could move, Stone jumped him and pointed his gun to his chest and fired once. Without wasting a moment, he stood and put Milla's body behind his to protect her from becoming a target.

Merrick turned and fired, hitting a man dead in the middle of his forehead. He dropped

like a heavy sack of potatoes. She shot her
way down the hallway. Milla flanked her, and
Stone moved to the front.

Toward the back of the house they
checked each room and came up empty. Merrick
was starting to wonder if they had slipped out
somehow. Stone signaled her to stop by
fisting his hand closed. She watched him nod
to confirm he found her mother and Maria.

Shots were fired, followed by a loud
crash, sending Stone rushing the room as he
dropped and rolled. Merrick rushed to the spot
Stone just vacated. She did a quick look and
watched Stone scan the room with his gun
raised. Merrick watched in slow motion as a
large man dressed in black backhanded her
mother across the face. The sound of Mom's
scream sent goose bumps down Merrick's spine.

How dare that motherfucker. Enraged,
Merrick shot him between the shoulder blades
more than once, but he must have been wearing
a vest because he slowly turned. Stone slid
across the floor in front of Merrick and shot
the huge man in the forehead. The attacker
dropped like a sack of potatoes.

"Watch out!" A man came out of nowhere
and was about to jump Stone, but Sal attacked
at a run, knocking them both to the ground in
hand-to-hand combat.

In the corner of the room Merrick caught
movement just as Gambino shot a man who came
through the French doors, dead Merrick heard
him snicker. At his feet her mother was
unconscious on the floor. Her mouth was
bloodied.

His pant's leg was torn, and he was
heavily bleeding, making it obvious to Merrick
that Fusion had attacked him at some point.
His clothes were ripped and torn, and where
the skin was exposed scratches and puncture
wounds were evident.

There was blood on her mother's clothes.
Merrick pulled off her mask. Her eyes moved up
from her mother to Gambino's face. Seething

with anger, she snarled. "You're going to die, you bastard."

Something in her expression must have scared him because Gambino took a step backward. Stone cleared the room of everyone else except Sal, who was releasing his wife from her ropes.

"This time you messed with the wrong person. All these years I waited and waited, hiding who I was and am because I wanted to get close enough to you to tear you and your business down." Merrick held a gun in each hand and pointed them at his head. She never took her eyes off of him.

Gambino moved swiftly, pulling her mother up against him as he put a mean blade to her throat. Her mother's head lolled back against his shoulder. "I'll slice her like an orange if you take another step. I'll kill her just like I killed your father," Gambino spat.

That made Merrick stop in her tracks, but she never lowered her guns. Where was Milla? She had made her a promise she wouldn't be the one to pull the trigger, but if Milla didn't hurry and take him out, Merrick would have no choice but to do it herself.

Movement outside the broken doorframe caught Merrick's attention. She spotted Milla as she moved silently as not to disturb the debris on the ground and make noise. Merrick raised her guns to indicate surrender. "Please don't hurt my mother." The foul taste of begging almost made her want to vomit, but she was playing for time. Milla was now in the house stealthily moving towards Gambino.

Stone moved to stand behind Merrick, and a few more men moved up behind Stone. Merrick felt them without having to look. All of them had their guns aimed, prepared to shoot. "Stand down," Merrick said. No one moved or listened.

Milla moved on silent feet, deadly fast and within a second she put her gun to Gambino's temple and shot. Blood and brain matter splattered all over the wall as Gambino's body fell limp to the floor.

Merrick ran to her mother's body, checking for a pulse. When she found it relief consumed her. After a quick inspection she realized her mother was going to be fine. She gathered her mom against her chest, feeling every bit thankful. Tears of relief ran unchecked down her cheeks.

When she looked up, Maria and Sal were approaching Milla who still held the gun in her hand. Maria touched her cheek, and Milla smiled into her mother's eyes. "I'm okay, Mom, really. I'm just a little shocked. It happened so fast. I sort of feel cheated because I couldn't tell him about himself, but he was going to hurt Merrick's mom and I couldn't allow that to happen. I thought I would feel something. Some kind of satisfaction, but there is only emptiness."

Sal took the gun from her fingers and stuck it into the waistband of his jeans. He pulled her into his embrace. "It's over, sweetheart."

Sirens blared, coming in fast. Merrick's mother eyes fluttered open. "Don't move, Mom, the paramedic's will be here any minute. You have been unconscious for a good few minutes so you need to be checked over."

Merrick brushed her hair from her face. "I love you, Mom. You're safe. It's over."

"Maria?" **She heard** her mother's voice raised in panic, as she tried to sit up.

"I'm right here."

Merrick watched Maria move to her mother's side and take her hand. "We're okay, Sis."

Police officers and two paramedics arrived, bursting through the open door. Everyone moved back to allow them access to Merrick's mother. Stone's arms went around Merrick, dragging her into his body. His warmth seeped into her giving her a sense of peace and but so much more. Total contentment. Something no pill could do, that's for sure.

One of the paramedic's stood up. "We're going to bring her in and make sure everything is fine. I think she needs a CT scan to make sure she doesn't have a concussion."

"You two can go home. I'll take care of the police," Sal said.

Merrick watched Maria cuddle her husband. She walked over to them and kissed them both. "I love you both so much!" Tears smarted behind her eyes. This was her family. Everything she ever counted on.

"Which home? Everything is a mess. We might have to get a hotel." Merrick shook her head as Stone started to guide her through the broken double doors.

"I'd like to try and stay at the house if we can." Stone hinted. "Maybe sleep out on the back deck on a blanket under the stars," he whispered in her ear.

She smiled. "Yes."

She turned her attention to Sal and Maria. "I can't believe this is all over. It seemed too easy. The FBI has their warrant for the Creole Kane Sugar Warehouse. They're bringing in the K-9's to assist the agents. It's all wrapped up. I'm not going to know what to do with myself." Merrick rubbed her forearms.

They were walking over towards the house cocooned in each others arms. Her cheek was against his chest as she listened to his heartbeat. She could see the firemen were still putting out the Aquarius. The pier was no longer on fire and would need to be repaired. What a day.

She had wondered how she would feel once Gambino was dead. Maybe it was too soon to tell. Everything felt surreal at the moment. Stone's fingers touched under her chin, tilting her face up. His lips touched hers softly. Awareness spiked through her body.

Fusion and Newton appeared by their sides, no worse for wear. Fusion's jaw was covered with blood. "Are you satisfied over the outcome of today, Mistress? Newton asked.

"Today I killed people. I'm not happy about that even if they were bad. It wasn't my place to decide if they lived or died, but they chose to attack my family and me. I had no choice but to defend my home and my loved ones. In the end, this will haunt me and give me nightmares. The only good thing is we won't have to live a double life anymore. My family can now live in peace, but I'm worried about Milla."

They walked through the broken French doors at the back of the house which looked like it had been turned upside down and shook hard. Everything was on the floor. Gambino's men had done this out of pure meanness, but this was just things. Things could be replaced.

"You expected this, right, Merrick? Don't allow this to get to you. We can fix whatever is broken.

"Don't take another step. This is now a crime scene. Please leave," police officer stated. "I'm about to tape off the house."

"Okay. I'm sorry I wasn't thinking." Merrick turned around with Stone to leave.

Stone guided her back outside to find Sal, Maria, and Milla standing in a circle.

"You've been evicted, too?" Merrick asked.

"Yes. They're taping off the house. I wasn't allowed to get any clothes or anything."

Milla hugged her mom gently. "It's ok, Mom. You all are coming to my house until we can figure things out. I have plenty of room."

"It's a deal. All I want is food, a shower, and a pillow. I'm starving and physically and mentally exhausted."

"Before Merrick and I follow I made a promise to a young lady. Before he could explain his unit showed up. One man limped, but they all looked tired. A few had blood over their clothes.

"Is anyone hurt? The paramedic's are still at the house. I could go get one before they leave." Merrick started to pull away from Stone. She looked them over trying to examine them.

"No, we're good. If one of us is hurt we doctor ourselves. We don't use public hospitals." The big man from earlier was the one who spoke. His voice was deep.

"Anyway, as soon as I handle this, we'll be there."

"What's going on?" The big man asked.

"I was telling them I made a promise to a teenager. Her mom is being threatened and beaten by the sounds of it, and I told her I'd be back. I need to keep this promise because no one has stepped up to help them."

"I'm coming. I'll stomp his ass."

"Ok, Hulk." Merrick giggled. "I'm sorry, I'm really tired.

"Milady, you can call me anything you wish. You're Stone's woman. That makes you part of this unit. We protect our own."

"Oh, thank you all for today." She walked up and hugged each person. "I appreciate everything you did today. I'll never forget it."

"I can't ask that of you guys," Stone interjected. "Today you went beyond the call of duty to help me out on the down low. I need to get them out of there immediately and teach this fucker a lesson he'll never forget and never think twice about looking for them."

The guys looked at each other and nodded their heads in agreement. "We're in!"

"We have to go to the bowling alley. It's where I met her. She doesn't believe I'll come back." He smiled. "I can't wait to see her face when we beat the shit out of her mother's boyfriend."

"Oh, you're not leaving me behind." Merrick was fired up. "What does she look like? Merrick questioned as she slid across Newton.

"Long blonde hair, about sixteen or seventeen, I think. She has dimples."

"Oh my stars. That sounds like Amy Gordon. We need to hurry I know her mom, Dana. She runs the bowling alley for me. That's bad because he's going to know where she works." Merrick added this information. "So your threats better come with a guarantee, fellows." Merrick pushed at Stone. "Hurry! I have to help her."

"We don't take kindly to assholes who put their hands on a woman," one of the other men spoke up. "Let's get this done. We'll follow behind you."

Sal and Maria hugged Merrick, "Don't take too long. We'll order pizza or something."

Merrick watched Milla kiss and hug her mom and dad.

"I want to come," Milla said.

"No, go take care of your parents. I have this. I might bring them back with us if that is okay with you, and tomorrow we'll figure things out.

"Sure! No problem."

"So just get enough food for everyone." Merrick hugged her tight. "I won't be long. Thank you, Sis."

Merrick walked back to Stone who pulled her under his arm, keeping her close. She loved the way he tucked her under his shoulder. The smell of him balanced all her senses. His alpha male made her feel safe. It was all pure bliss.

Newton materialized with Fusion at his side. "Thank you both for everything. Fusion girl, I would love it if you stayed behind and guard mom, Maria, and Milla. I just want to make sure, if any of Gambino's men feel up to a surprise attack, they have proper protection. Sal is exhausted. Would you do that for me, Girl?"

Fusion turned and ran off toward the others. "She said she will contact me if anything happen," Newton stated.

As they drove into the night, Merrick watched their back just in case any of Gambino's men found out Gambino was dead. Two black SUV's were following behind them. Merrick knew Dana's boyfriend was in big trouble.

The ride took a little over an hour by motorcycle and truck. "Drive past the bowling alley. She lives about two blocks down on Bishop St. Third house on the left."

Newton quieted the vehicle's approach and pulled up close to the residence. Someone was yelling in the house, and it was around three A.M. in the morning. Stone looked back at Merrick and waited for her to get off. He slid off and made his way to the truck.

"Team one, I want you around the back entrance. In ten minutes hit the power until the count of five, and then turn it back on. On signal enter. I would like this to be a surprise entrance. I want to see his face when I jerk his ass up," Stone commanded.

"Team two, enter through the side door and wait for my signal. Be careful of the children. Team three you're with me. Signal me when you find the girl child."

Within minutes the signal came, and Merrick and Stone moved quickly to the girl's bedroom window and gently knocked. The blond-headed girl cautiously peeked around the curtain to see who was there. When she saw Stone, she smiled widely and opened the window.

"You came," she whispered. "With help?"

"No, little lady, with the calvary."

She opened the window wider to let them enter.

Stone whistled a signal before he crawled through. "Here is a small flash light so you can see. Pack a bag of what's most important to you because you won't be coming back here. Got it?"

The young girl grabbed her school bad and a backpack and started throwing clothes in. The yelling increased in the living room.

"Let's move! The others will be indoors by now." The lights went out and Stone rushed into the living room. Stone moved to stand in front of the drunk man just as the lights came back on.

"What are you doing in my house?" the drunk man screamed.

"I needed to pick up a few things, then I'll be on my way."

"There is nothing here for you, mister. See your fucking ass out before I show you out."

In the midst of the yelling, the daughter showed up with her bags packed and another bag for her mother.

"Where the fuck do you think you're going, young lady?"

"She and her mother Dana will be leaving with me. They will not return and you will not go looking for them," The big man named Bear on Stone's team told him.

"Oh, hell to the no! Dana is my girlfriend and she stays here." The drunk moved to grab her and pull her around Stone's body, but Bear picked him up off the ground so his feet dangled. He shoved him against the wall.

"I don't think you heard me too well. You might be stupid or something. Let me try a different tactic." He pulled out a wicked-looking blade and put it under to the drunk's chin. "If you try to contact her or go to her job or anything, if I hear anything that you might be searching for them, I'm going to come back and filet you like a big juicy red fish."

"Put him down," Stone commanded.

The big guy released his grip and let the man fall.

Stone punched him hard in the stomach, knocking the air from the man's lungs. A different man on the team pulled him from Stone and into his reach and grabbed a fistful of hair and yanked his head back and licked his face.

"Give him to me, Boss," the man pleaded. "Pretty please."

"No! Don't give me to him." The boyfriend begged. The men pushed him from one to the other. Everyone who caught him, beat on him. The boyfriend had lost all sense of control. His nose was broken, his eyes were swollen, and his lip was cut.

The floors seem to tremble when the biggest man came from the back of the house. He was massive and when he took a step the floor boards felt like they were about to give way.

"These two are mine now. You understand?" The massive man picked the boyfriend up by his throat with one hand and with the other grabbed a handful of his hair and pulled it back to front. "Say yes." He jerked the boyfriend's head like a puppet.

"Yes!Yes!Yes! Just stay away from me."

"If we have to come back, we will kill you and put your body out for the alligators.

"Listen!" One of the men standing in the back yelled. "Quiet!"

The television was on, and the late evening newscaster was standing outside of the yellow taped off area, broadcasting live. The newsman stated, "Crime lord Anthony Gambino has been found dead. His whole personal entourage as well as the well-known Sharkman and his right-hand man, have also been found dead."

The newscaster went on to say. "Rumor has it that his only son who lives in Italy will be flying in for the service. There isn't any mention of any successor at this time of who will take over the family business."

"Son? Gambino has a son? Oh my god." Merrick sat down hard on the sofa. "This can't be happening." She put her head in her hands. "All of this was for nothing?" She saw Stone's legs move in close so she looked up.

Merrick watched Stone reach his hand out for hers. She put her hand in his and allowed him to pull her up. Her hands fisted in his shirt. Her legs felt like rubber.

"Do you guys know anything about this? Milla has a brother?"

The big guy punched the drunk across the face to knock him out.

"Are you two ladies ready for a new beginning?"

"Yes", they both quoted.

"Let's get out of here so we can regroup," Stone commanded.

"Make sure you have all of your important papers, anything special you want to bring because the two of you won't ever see this place again."

The blond-head young girl named Amy threw herself at Stone in a huge bear hug. "You didn't forget me."

Merrick could hear the girl crying silently.

"Yes, we're family, right, big guy?"

"I always wanted a little sister. Call me Clint, or the guys call me Hulk. Whatever you feel comfortable with."

Merrick felt Stone pull her from the house. Obviously she could feel shock wanting to drag her down. "I am not free. Neither is Mom, Maria or Sal or Milla."

"Let's head out. We'll need to talk with Sal and everyone and see what our next plan will be. Until then, it's you and me, baby. I love you," Stone whispered.

"I love you more," Merrick whispered back. She went into his embrace, craving his touch.

"Well, little lady, you're going to have to prove it to me everyday for the rest of your life. I won't take no for an answer," Stone stated. "We're getting married tomorrow."

Made in the USA
Columbia, SC
16 August 2018